As much as Julian Allard has enjoyed the trip to Las Vegas, he's more than ready to head home. While on vacation, his coven master, Jean-Paul, found his beloved—the other half of his soul—making his task of security that much harder. Julian wants to get Jean-Paul and his human, Saul, home to the safety of their territory.

At the airport, Julian feels the need to do one more sweep of the area. Never second-guessing his instincts, he does just that. Near the back of the hangar, Julian sees a human backhand another, who's handling a baggage cart. The smell of the fallen human's blood draws Julian, and he rushes to his side, scaring away the unconscious man's attacker.

A quick taste of the human's blood confirms Julian's suspicions. The pretty red-haired human is his beloved. Acting on impulse, Julian sweeps the human into his arms and rushes him onto their private jet. Even as Julian cares for his unconscious new and forever love, can he figure out a way to explain, well . . . everything?

Kidnapping the Baggage Boy

ISBN: 978-1-4874-3941-5
Cover art by Angela Waters

Published by eXtasy Books Inc

Look for us online at:
www.eXtasybooks.com

Kidnapping the Baggage Boy
A Loving Nip: 31

By

Charlie Richards

Dedication

If nothing ever changed, there'd be no butterflies.
~Unknown

CHAPTER ONE

"Are you ready to go, my beloved?"

"As ready as I'll ever be."

As Julian Allard zipped his suitcase closed, he listened to the two men speaking in the second bedroom of their two-bedroom hotel suite. He and his coven master, Jean-Paul Tremblay, had arrived in Las Vegas nearly three weeks before. They'd originally only planned to stay a week, but that had all changed when, on the first night of their visit, Jean-Paul had stumbled across his beloved in a wine bar.

Jean-Paul had made quick work of wooing Saul Mandisa, not that the human had tried to play hard to get. Saul had even handled the whole *paranormals are real and I'm a vampire* reveal with amazing ease. The mate-pull sure had been working hard for Master Jean-Paul that day.

Julian was happy for the pair. Truly, he was. If at night, when he went to bed and his arms were empty while hearing soft croons from across the way—the hotel rooms weren't totally sound-proofed against a vampire's exceptional hearing—Julian did his best to ignore his jealousy.

Saul wasn't Julian's type anyway. He just wished he could find his own beloved—the other half of his soul. A vampire's beloved was the one person on earth that they could bond with, connecting their life-threads and giving them someone to spend their long, sometimes five-hundred-year-old life with.

Closing in on the three-hundred-year-old mark, Julian had waited a long time.

But now my coven master has found his beloved. That gives me hope that Fate is finally smiling upon us.

With that thought in mind, Julian hefted his suitcase off the bed and placed it on the floor. He extended the handle, tipped the case, and began rolling it out of the room that had been his home for the last number of days. He looked forward to heading home. While Las Vegas held many attractions, the fact that so many tourists filled the streets, casinos, and other venues damn near twenty-four-seven, had made security a living nightmare.

Julian was their vampire coven's head enforcer, and he took the safety of the master very seriously. They'd been there to meet up with a few vampire friends and their beloveds, so he hadn't thought extra security would be necessary. That had been before Jean-Paul had found his beloved.

Can't wait to get them both home to the safety of our coven in Montpellier, France.

The hot desert was definitely getting to Julian, too. He longed for the cooler climate of his home, and he missed the scent of the sea. Tourists were a fact of life in Montpellier, too, but their coven home was situated in the hills above the city, surrounded by rolling hills covered in vineyards.

Blessed solitude.

After leaving his suitcase in the foyer of the two-bedroom suite, Julian returned to his room. He did a quick sweep of the room and the attached ensuite to make certain he hadn't inadvertently forgotten something. He hadn't. Julian did the same for the shared rooms, too.

By the time Julian finished his double-check, Master Jean-Paul and Saul were waiting for him in the foyer.

"Ready, Julian?" Jean-Paul asked with a quirk of his dark eyebrow.

Julian nodded once. "Yes." With a soft chuckle as he pulled the door open for his master, he added, "And if we missed something, it probably wasn't important anyway."

Jean-Paul smirked. "Indeed." With his hand resting on Saul's lower back and his other holding the handle of his suitcase, he urged his beloved out of the suite. In a soft purr, he murmured, "I look forward to showing you my home, beloved."

"Can't wait to see it," the laid-back human replied, flashing a smile at Jean-Paul. He rolled a brand-new suitcase of his own behind him, compliments of Jean-Paul. "How long is the flight?"

As Jean-Paul answered, Julian tossed their key cards onto the side table. They'd already checked out via telephone. Then he grabbed the handle of his own suitcase and left the suite, anticipation filling him.

Just as Julian had requested from the valet, a town car was waiting at the front door to drive them to the airport.

Twenty-five minutes of Las Vegas traffic later, the town car traveled through the guard gate leading to a private hangar. There was absolutely no way Julian would allow his coven master to board a commercial aircraft. Instead, they utilized the services of a charter service.

The car stopped before the hangar, and Julian exited first. He did a quick visual sweep of the area, searching for danger. While his vampire senses felt on alert for some reason, he couldn't spot anything amiss.

After a second of hesitation, Julian eased away from the door and allowed his charges to exit. "I'll be right back for the luggage," he told the driver. "Please stay in the vehicle."

"Yes, sir," the human replied, although he looked a little surprised at the order.

Julian figured the man usually unloaded the luggage. He'd helped them load it, after all. With his senses on high alert, Julian didn't want to give the man a chance to slip any explosives or whatnot into their luggage.

Paranoid much?

Except, something is bothering me.

Julian always trusted his instincts.

Once Julian had escorted Jean-Paul and Saul to the plane, he stepped into the cockpit to talk to the pilot. The man—a human—was already seated at the controls and appeared to be doing paperwork or a pre-flight check. Julian wasn't a pilot, so he could only guess.

"How are we looking?" Julian asked. "Will we be ready to leave soon?"

The pilot lifted his head from his work, turning to look at him with clear blue eyes. "Yes, sir," he replied. "I'm just waiting for clearance and what strip to use." After a glance at his instruments, the man returned his focus to him. "Probably less than ten minutes."

"Good." Julian really was ready to get home. "I need to grab our luggage and stow it. Be right back."

"Do you need any help, sir?" The human set his clipboard aside and made as if to rise.

Julian shook his head as he waved off the offer. "No. It'll only take me a minute."

Without waiting for a response, Julian exited the cockpit, then the plane. The town car was waiting right where he'd left it. The driver's attention was on his phone, but as soon as Julian tapped the side of the vehicle with a knuckle, his head came up. Then the man popped the trunk.

After removing the luggage and setting it aside, Julian moved to the window. "Thanks for the lift," he stated, offering the man a folded-up hundred-dollar bill.

The driver grinned at him, taking the tip. "My pleasure, sir. Have a safe flight."

Julian nodded as he stepped backward, watching the guy roll up his window. After crossing to their bags, he easily hefted the several cases. Just as he reached the base of the stairs, Julian heard the murmur of voices toward the back of the hangar.

The melodious tenor of the first voice caused his gut to warm. He would have ignored it if the second voice didn't sound so angry. A strange burning need to check out the situation surged through him.

Taking the steps two at a time, Julian deposited the luggage into the cabin. "Be right back, Jean-Paul," he told his master, who was sitting beside Saul in one of the thick-cushioned recliners.

Even though Jean-Paul arched a brow in silent question, Julian didn't take the time to answer. He rushed back down the stairs and began rounding the plane. On silent feet, Julian headed toward the voices.

"Look, I need the money back for gas for the week, Morgan," the tenor voice stated, his voice sounding smooth and even. "You said you'd have it back to me last Thursday, remember?"

"I ain't givin' you shit back," the other man replied darkly. "And there ain't nothin' you can do about it."

As Julian slipped under the wing of another plane, the speakers came into view. A pretty redhead in khaki shorts with an orange safety vest over his polo stood beside a baggage cart half-full of suitcases, one freckled hand resting on the metal upright. His brows were drawn, and he looked to be barely keeping his frustration off his features.

"Look," the redhead began again. "I gave you that money in good faith. I—"

The other man stood a couple of inches taller and was broader than the baggage boy. "What you got is sucker written on your forehead." As he spoke, he poked the redhead in the forehead. "Now get outta my way."

That was when Julian realized the baggage boy seemed to be using his cart to block the door.

"No," the smaller man replied, tipping his chin up stubbornly. His eyes narrowed, and he scowled at the guy.

"You—"

"Don't give a shit, faggot."

A second later, the bigger man backhanded the redhead. Letting out a surprised hiss, the smaller man stumbled backward. His left foot caught on the wheel of his cart, and the hold he had on the upright caused his body to twist as he fell. His head slammed into the railing, and he lost his grip on the cart.

Even before the pretty man had completely crumpled to the hard ground, Julian began rushing forward. He growled when the big man cackled, pulled back his steel-toed boot, and slammed it into the back of the fallen man's head. The redhead lay still.

Just as the man began pulling his foot back for another blow, Julian snarled, "Hey!"

The man froze, snapping his attention to Julian. In the next instant, he shoved the cart aside and rushed out the door.

As tempted as Julian was to give chase to the asshole, the fragrant scent of the redhead's blood blossomed in the air. He skidded to a stop beside the downed man, his heart rate accelerating in his chest. Inhaling again, Julian couldn't stop the soft moan from escaping him.

Delicious.

Julian's mouth watered for a taste of the fragrant goodness. Spotting the bloom of red that began pooling near the back of the human's head, he couldn't help himself. He reached out a trembling hand and swiped his first two fingers along the red goodness darkening the spikey strands.

Lifting his digits to his mouth, Julian slipped them between his lips. The second the iron-rich fluid hit his tongue, his taste buds damn near exploded. The O-negative fluid caused his senses to sing, and his cock went from zero to hard as steel in two seconds flat.

"Beloved," Julian hissed, shock flooding him.

He could hardly believe it. His brain froze with the

knowledge. Lying prone on the floor before him was the other half of his soul.

"Julian?" Jean-Paul's voice echoed through the hangar. "Where are you? We've received clearance. We need to leave."

Leave? No.

I can't leave my beloved.

"Coming!" Julian called. Making a snap decision, he scooped his bleeding beloved into his arms. He sprinted to their plane and bounded up the steps.

Pausing within the cabin, Julian saw the pilot to his right beside the door. He'd evidently been getting ready to close it. When the pilot's attention fell on the bleeding man, he opened his mouth.

Julian cut him off. Hazing his eyes, he pushed mentally into the pilot's mind. He noticed the way the human's expression blanked just a little, and he knew he'd connected.

"Our fourth passenger managed to make it, after all," Julian told him. "Everything is well."

"Everything is well," the pilot parroted, his mind under Julian's influence.

"We can leave now," Julian added.

The pilot nodded, blinking slowly. "We'll leave now."

Pulling out of the pilot's mind, Julian watched the man blink once more before turning his attention to the stairs and began closing the door.

Julian didn't bother watching. He rushed through the cabin toward the back. He knew their charter plane had a small bedroom in the back. Once inside, he carefully laid his unconscious beloved on the bed, grimacing when the man's head sank into the soft pillow and he moaned.

"Easy, beloved," Julian crooned in his native French, running his hand down the side of the man's face. Resting on the side of the bed, he softly added, "You're safe, handsome. I promise."

As the plane began moving, Julian heard Saul say, "Did Julian just bring someone on board?"

"Yes." Jean-Paul's voice held an uncharacteristic amount of shock. "Yes, he did."

Saul cleared his throat once, then asked, "Are we kidnapping someone?"

"Yes." Jean-Paul still sounded amazed. "Yes, I believe we are."

As the plane lifted into the air, Julian finally realized what he'd just done.

Gods, how will I ever explain this to my beloved?

Chapter Two

A dull ache throbbed through Teason Lofgren's head, and he bit back a moan. He breathed slowly, trying to work through the pain. Teason also tried to figure out why he hurt so much because it wasn't just in his head.

Slowly, Teason cataloged the various aches pulsing through him. The back of his head seemed to be the worst of it, but there was also an ache in his left shoulder. It sort of felt as if he'd wrenched it.

Did I fall and hit my head?

Just as fast as the thought entered his mind, a sharp memory of Morgan backhanding him flashed through his brain.

Yep, definitely fell.

God, what an asshole.

How did I fall for his weaselly good-ol-boy routine?

Teason was normally a better judge of character. Having lived mostly on his own from the age of sixteen, he'd had to grow up pretty quick.

Not that Mom stopped loving me.

She just couldn't . . .

The low rumble of voices drew Teason's attention. That was followed by the realization that he lay on his stomach on something soft. It felt far softer than what Teason imagined a hospital bed would feel.

Cracking open his eyelids, Teason noticed the lights were dimmed. That didn't stop him from making out narrow furniture. It reminded him of something that one would find in a camper or recreational vehicle.

Except, the finishes appeared really . . . *nice.*

Definitely not a hospital.

Then where?

Doing his best to ignore the throb in his head and the ache in his shoulder, Teason focused on the low rumble of voices. It took him a minute to realize that the men weren't speaking English. After listening to the words for a few seconds, he realized it was French, and he began to pick up bits and pieces.

"Damn, Julian," a soft tenor whispered harshly. "What were you . . ."

"The man is my . . . I could not leave him."

Oh, that's a nice deep voice. I could listen to his gorgeous accent all day.

Yep. I've definitely hit my head.

"Your . . ." The first man sounded surprised. "You are . . ."

"Yes," the second one replied, a deep sigh escaping him. "I tasted his . . ."

Slowly, his years of being friends with a French foreign exchange student, of learning the language and conversing with him, helped his brain sort out even more.

"I want to congratulate you, Julian," the first man stated. "Truly, I do. But . . . you . . . him."

"I did not think of it as . . ." the second man responded, sounding a mixture of earnest and upset—Julian. *Sexy name.* "He was . . . I could not ask him. I tasted him. He is mine. I . . ."

"Dude, Julian," another deep voice cut in, although he sounded amused. He was also speaking English. "I can't understand most of what you vamps are sayin', but I sure wish I had some popcorn when your beloved wakes up." He rumbled a deep laugh before adding, "What a hell of a way to be introduced to paranormals." Without missing a beat, the guy continued, "Hey, I bet you'll be the first vampire to claim his beloved and join the mile-high club at the same time."

Vamps. Paranormals. Vampires.

Well, shit.

Teason knew that vampires existed, but he'd never met any before. At least, not that he was aware of, anyway. It wasn't as if a human could look at one and know.

Unease slithered through him.

Why would a vampire take me to . . . wherever I am?

Julian sounded as if he were sighing deeply, and Teason barely made out his soft response of, "Thank you, Saul. I appreciate it." Julian had switched to English, probably for Saul's benefit. "Maybe you could, uh, help me explain?"

"I'm happy to help, man," Saul responded.

"When the young human wakes, we'll both do our best to help him stay calm," the first man commented, having also switched to English. "Thirty-thousand feet is no place to panic."

"Thank you, Jean-Paul," Julian responded.

Wait a minute. Thirty-thousand feet?

Then Teason's attention snagged on Saul's quip about the mile-high club.

Holy shit. Am I on a plane?

Pushing to his elbows, Teason hissed as pain spiked through not only his shoulder but his head. Spots danced before his eyes. Blinking rapidly, he did his best to ignore them so he could survey the room.

"Whoa, easy." The deep-voiced male—a vampire, Teason guessed—rushed into the room. His wide shoulders spanned the distance of the doorway as he entered. "Don't try to get up yet," he encouraged, his hands lifted in placation. "You've been injured."

"I know," Teason grumbled. "Damn Morgan," he snarled even as he lowered back to his chest.

Just talking hurt, and he realized his throat was damn dry. Eyeing the guy who was nearing the bed, his movements slow as if he were approaching a skittish horse, Teason wondered if he should reveal that he'd heard their conversation and understood, well, some of it, anyway.

"My name is Julian Allard, not Morgan," the big, dark-haired man told him, obviously misunderstanding. "I saw that other man attack you. You fell and hit your head." A low growl escaped him as he added, "Then the asshole kicked you in the head." His hands clenched and released as if he were imagining hitting the man. "He ran when I approached."

"Sooo, you decided to take me on a plane ride instead of calling the cops?" Teason asked softly, deciding to keep his yap shut about his knowledge of paranormals.

Teason wanted to know what these men would admit to him. After all, knowledge was power. Would they truly admit to being vampires, and if so, he wondered why.

"I, uh." Julian rubbed the back of his neck, suddenly looking sheepish. "I acted rashly."

Even though Teason thought the uncertain look on Julian looked completely out of place, it was cute . . . sort of. He would bet the big man rarely admitted to acting without thinking. Teason just thought the man had the baring of someone who normally exuded confidence . . . especially judging by his high-end suit.

"Um, water?" Teason asked softly, hoping to buy a few seconds to think.

Plus, seeing how Julian acted toward his request might help Teason figure out if he was a captive or not.

"Oh, yes. Of course." Julian took a couple of steps backward as he cautioned, "Stay still, and don't touch the bandage on your head, please."

Resting his cheek on the pillow, Teason nodded once. Of course, as soon as Julian fled the room, he immediately lifted a hand to his head. Teason gently felt around the area of his head that caused the most pain, barely biting back a hiss.

"Damn it, beloved," Julian muttered, reappearing in the

doorway way faster than Teason had expected. "I said *don't* touch your head."

Even as Julian scolded him, he hurried to Teason and settled on the side of the bed. "The plane only had a few large bandages in the first aid kit," he continued, almost as if he were rambling. At the same time, Julian twisted the cap on the water bottle. The crack-pop noise told Teason that it had been sealed. "They don't affix very good to your hair, and your head wound was bleeding pretty badly. I hope there'll be enough to last the trip." As Julian continued to speak, he cradled Teason's jaw in a surprisingly gentle hold. "Small sips to start."

Julian held the water bottle to his lips and tipped it. Some of it went into his mouth, but even more dribbled out the other side. Julian didn't seem concerned about the mess as he continued to help him take small mouthfuls.

Teason found the move surprisingly intimate, and the hairs on his neck stood on end. He had to concentrate on focusing on the cool water and not the strong hand beneath his cheek. When Julian stroked his thumb over Teason's flesh, he nearly choked.

Pulling back, Teason managed to swallow the mouthful. He cleared his throat, then murmured, "Well, you know how it is? Tell someone not to look up, and that's exactly what they do."

A low chuckle rumbled from Julian, and Teason felt his stomach clench upon hearing the sound.

"Very true."

As Teason watched, Julian eased onto the bed beside him. The man—vampire—put his back to the headboard. Resting the open bottle on his upturned knee, he furrowed his brows for a second, his expression going a little vacant.

Then Julian blinked and returned his focus to Teason. "I'm sorry. I should have asked." With a rueful grimace, he offered,

"There's *ibuprofen* in the first aid kit. Does anything hurt besides your head?" Julian reached out and touched Teason's temple.

Unable to help himself, Teason jerked back from Julian's touch. It wasn't that he didn't want the man to touch him. Just the opposite, in fact. Teason didn't know why, but he liked it a little too much.

Julian yanked his hand back, his dark eyes going wide. "I would never hurt you," he whispered roughly.

To Teason's surprise, Julian actually looked . . . upset . . . that he'd pulled away.

"Sorry," Teason muttered. Although, he wasn't totally certain what he was apologizing for. Thinking quickly, he asked, "So, uh . . . can I ask where we're headed?"

"France," Julian replied, shocking Teason. "Paris first, then Montpellier."

"Holy fuck," Teason whispered. "France?"

Teason could only gape at the man as shock flooded his system.

How the hell –

"Easy, easy. You're safe. I promise."

Julian crooned the words, but Teason could hardly process them.

France! How can I get away from vampires in France?

"You're okay, *ma adorée*. You're safe. Hush, *ma adorée*. I've got you."

Slowly, Teason registered the warmth of a big body plastered along his own. He felt strong arms holding him. Huge hands rubbed up and down his back soothingly.

Teason sucked in a harsh breath and nearly moaned. The vampire's delicious aroma flooded his senses. He smelled of a fresh masculine scent, something a little spicy and wild, along with something Teason couldn't quite place. Altogether, it caused his arousal to soar, and he felt his prick harden despite his pain and panic.

Holy shit! What the hell?

In the next instant, Teason realized Julian had sprawled next to him at some point. The much bigger male was holding him in his arms. The vampire had draped Teason's body halfway across his own torso, and his hands rubbed up and down Teason's back soothingly.

All the while, Julian continued to croon nonsense about how Teason was safe and everything would be okay and how he would never hurt him.

Teason actually found himself reacting . . . relaxing even as his body heated with arousal.

Only one reason for his responses made sense to Teason.

Freezing in Julian's grip, Teason peered at him. "Am I in some kind of vampire thrall?"

Julian stopped midsentence. His lips were parted in obvious surprise for one second, then two. Then Julian's eyes widened, even as a slight smile curved his full lips.

"You know of vampires?" Julian's lips widened into a broader smile, and just the tips of his fangs could be seen between his parted lips. "How, *ma adorée*?"

Oh, shit. I shouldn't have said that.

A new, cold tingle of panic trickled up Teason's spine.

Chapter Three

Julian couldn't have been more shocked if Teason had run through the cabin naked, yanked open the emergency exit, and jumped from the plane without a parachute.

My beloved knows of vampires?

Mmmm . . . a naked Teason.

Then the fresh scent of panic tickled Julian's nostrils, and he yanked his attention back to where it needed to be—assuring Teason of his safety.

"Relax, *ma adorée,*" Julian crooned, continuing to rub his hands up and down Teason's back. Then Teason's actual question registered, and Julian quickly reassured, "No, Teason. You're not captured by a vampire thrall. Although most of us refer to it as trancing someone."

To Julian's relief, he felt Teason begin to relax against him. The hand that was resting on Julian's chest twitched. He felt the scrape of his fingernails even through his shirt, and desperately wondered what they would feel like against his skin. Julian's nipples even beaded, as if in anticipation.

"Th-Then why, uh . . ." Teason snapped his mouth shut for a second. His auburn brows furrowed, and he peered at Julian through his lashes. "H-How do you kn-know my name?"

Julian smiled at Teason. While he didn't like why he'd ended up needing to hold his beloved, he would happily do it for any reason. The feel of his human tucked into his arms and pressed against his body had a predictable reaction on his libido, but he did his best to ignore his hard prick.

After all, they still had plenty to talk about.

"From your driver's license," Julian told him. He glanced at the tiny nightstand situated to the bed's left. "I put it and the other items from your pockets into the drawer there." Returning his focus to Teason, Julian teased his fingertips over his human's spine. "That way, if we ran into turbulence, nothing would go anywhere."

"Oh."

Teason whispered the word so softly, Julian knew if he hadn't been a vampire, he wouldn't have heard it. The move did bring his attention to Teason's lips. Julian instinctively licked his own as he wondered how that plump flesh would taste.

"Um, so." Teason paused and cleared his throat. When Julian returned his attention to his human's eyes, Teason's cheeks had taken on a pinkish hue, and his beloved was staring at Julian's chest. "So, n-not a thrall. Then, um, why . . . why are you holding me? A-And why am I-I liking it so much?" Teason's scowl looked almost vacant, as if he were thinking hard. "Shouldn't I be trying to figure out how to get away? Except, I'm on a plane. How could I?" Finally, Teason snapped his gaze back to Julian's face. "Is that why you took me on a plane? So you could drain me dry without anyone knowing the wiser?"

Julian hated that *that* was the conclusion that Teason jumped to. It made him wonder just how—and from whom—his beloved had learned of vampires.

Just what garbage has my beloved's mind been filled with?

Knowing the only way to find out was to ask, Julian reminded Teason, "I already told you I would never harm you. Nor will I allow another to harm you." He fought against a blush as he added, "I told you I acted rashly by bringing you on board when you were injured. The reason for that is because when I tasted your blood in the garage, I realized you were my beloved."

"Your beloved?" A look of confusion crossed Teason's face.

"I, uh, I don't know what that means." Tensing in Julian's arms, he whispered, "You already tasted my blood? You bit me? Does that mean I'm going to turn into a vampire, too?"

Huh. Okay.

"Where did you learn of paranormals, Teason?" Julian pressed softly. "It's rare a human knows of us, let alone can recognize us on sight as you have me."

Just how the hell did Teason even realize I'm a vampire?

"I, uh, I heard you and the other guys talking in the hall," Teason admitted, swallowing so hard his Adam's apple bobbed. "I knew that other guy, uh, Saul, I think, was telling the truth because I know you guys exist."

Once again, Julian simply asked, "How?"

After staring at Julian for a long moment, Teason told him, "My mom is mated with a lion shifter."

"Really?" Julian couldn't help but grin. "So you lived with their pride for a while? You learned about paranormals from them?" That made a bit more sense, except—"Except, they did a piss-poor job of explaining vampires to you."

"Uh, no." Teason shook his head a little, his cheek rubbing on Julian's chest distractingly. "No, I never lived with them."

"Ooookay." A fresh bout of confusion filled Julian, and he felt as if he had more questions with every answer he received. "If you don't mind, let's start at the beginning." Knowing he wouldn't get answers if he didn't provide some of his own, Julian decided to go with, "Just like shifters, vampires are born, not made. I didn't bite you. You were bleeding, and you smelled so good that I couldn't resist tasting it." Unable to help but smile as he recalled the exquisite flavor of Teason's blood, Julian hummed. "Gods, you taste amazing, Teason, and in that instant, I knew you were *ma adorée*."

"And that is?" Teason questioned hesitantly.

"My beloved, adored, cherished," Julian crooned, offering a couple of possible translations for his endearment. Recalling the fact that, somehow, Teason had learned about paranormals from shifters, Julian explained, "A beloved to a vampire is like a mate to a shifter. You are the other half of my soul." Excitement and anticipation flooded Julian as he rubbed his palm down Teason's side. "You are the one person on this planet I can bond with, and I will treasure you forever."

"Oh, damn." Teason stared up at him with wide hazel eyes that seemed to glitter beautifully in the dim cabin lighting. "Really?"

Julian offered Teason a sensual smile. "*Really.*"

Seeing Teason's mouth open, then close, then open again, Julian couldn't resist closing the distance between them. He needed a taste so badly. Moving slowly, Julian drew closer, his attention flicking from Teason's eyes to his lips and back again, giving his human plenty of time to draw away or tell him no if he so chose.

To Julian's relief—and pleasure—Teason didn't. His nostrils flared slightly, and his hazel eyes dilated. He even tilted his chin up in offering.

Perfect.

Sealing his lips over Teason's, Julian licked and nibbled lightly at the plump flesh. He hummed with delight upon tasting his beloved's flavor. With a nip to Teason's bottom lip, his beloved quickly opened to him.

Julian immediately accepted that invitation and slipped his tongue into Teason's mouth. His beloved's masculine flavor burst across his taste buds, touched with a hint of mint and . . . ginger. Julian delved deeper as his blood fired in his veins, lapping at Teason's appendage, enjoying the way he returned the tongue-play.

Wanting closer, deeper, Julian tightened the arm he had wrapped around Teason's waist. He slid his other up his side to his nape. Julian slipped his fingers into the hair at Teason's nape, intending to urge his beloved to tilt his head so he could deepen the kiss.

Just as his fingers tugged at the side of the bandage, Teason jerked back with a hiss.

"Ah, *zut alors,*" Julian cursed in French as he yanked his hand from Teason's hair. "Forgive me, *ma adorée.*" Grimacing as he peered into Teason's wincing features, he admitted, "I lost myself in your amazing taste. It will not happen again."

Teason blew out a breath as he touched his head. Nibbling his bottom lip for a second, he peered at Julian through his lashes. Then, to Julian's surprise, Teason smirked.

"I sure hope you don't mean that."

Confused, Julian cocked his head. "I never wish to hurt you, Teason," he told him. "Of course, I mean it."

"Except, I like that you lost control because of me, forgetting that I'm injured," Teason told him softly. After another wince, he lowered his hand. "But you're right that now isn't the time." After another second, Teason admitted, "And I do have some questions."

"Understandable," Julian replied, resting his hand against Teason's neck and massaging lightly. "Just as I have questions for you."

Teason blew out a breath. "Yeah. Uh, okay."

Realizing Teason was just too much of a temptation while cuddling together, Julian eased away a little. "Shall we sit up?" he asked upon seeing his human's questioning look. "I can also get us a snack." Julian glanced at his watch. "We still have many hours before we make Paris."

"How long was I out?" Teason asked, accepting Julian's help to rise to a sitting position.

As Julian helped Teason rest against the headboard, pillows surrounding him for comfort and stability, he told him, "About four hours. Long enough for us to land, refuel, and head out again. We're over the Atlantic now." While he didn't usually express his feelings to others—he was the head enforcer of his vampire coven, after all—Julian didn't bother to hide them from his beloved. "You had me worried. I wanted to heal your wound and skip the bandage, but Saul said that might seem a little odd and hard to explain to you. Especially if you didn't remember getting injured."

"Yeah, well, I remember," Teason told him, relaxing against the pillows. Resting his hands on his upturned knees, he cocked his head. "How would you have healed me?" Before Julian could answer, he heard Teason's stomach growl, and his beloved's cheeks took on a pinkish hue. "Uh, and a snack would be great. I'm guessing lunch was quite some time ago."

"Vegas time lunch? Yes," Julian confirmed with a chuckle. Leaning close, he pecked a kiss to Teason's lips because, even if he could resist, he didn't want to try. "Are you allergic to anything?"

"Uh, the oils on zucchini skin."

Julian straightened, surprise filling him. "Really?" When Teason pressed his lips together in a firm line and nodded once, Julian asked, "How'd you find that out?"

"Mom had a garden when I was growing up," Teason told him readily, pleasing Julian with his openness. "She decided to grow zucchini one year. We ended up with a dozen, and she thought it'd be fun to make fried zucchini sticks." Teason chuckled softly even as he shook his head. "I helped her by using a carrot peeler to remove the skin, and she cut it up and fried it. Tasted amazing." With a wince, Teason scratched his chest as his eyes grew a little vacant, perhaps with remembered pain, as he murmured, "I ended up with hives over my chest, stomach, arms, and thighs, and it took us forever to figure out what caused them."

"How did you?" Julian asked curiously.

"Internet searches and process of elimination," Teason told him, meeting his gaze. With a half-shrug, he added, "Handling zucchini was the only thing in my life that had changed.

No new laundry detergent. No new soaps or body washes. Surprisingly, the allergy is pretty common."

"Why over your body and not just your arms and hands?" While Julian believed Teason—his beloved's scent certainly confirmed that the human believed it—he found it a little odd.

With a bark of laughter, Teason told him, "I was twelve. I'd wiped my hands on my shirt and shorts, and the oil soaked through . . . everywhere."

Wincing in sympathy, Julian nodded as he slipped from the bed. "No handling zucchini for you." He cocked his head as he admitted, "Although, I don't think that's something we grow in our greenhouse. We do have other squashes, though." Julian focused on Teason as he began backing out of the room. "Any other plant oils bother you?"

"Not that I'm aware of yet."

Julian nodded. "Be right back." Then he hurried from the room, vowing to keep an eye on Teason if he ended up helping harvest their fruits and vegetables.

Stopping at the back of the cabin where a small kitchenette was tucked, Julian began rummaging through the mini-fridge and cupboards.

"So Teason knows about us." Jean-Paul stopped beside him, leaning his butt against a nearby chair. "That's . . . fortuitous."

"It is," Julian acknowledged, choosing a small turkey sandwich from the fridge, as well as a single-serving bottle of white wine and a soda. Straightening, he turned to face his coven master. "Fate has truly blessed me."

"That she has." Jean-Paul smiled widely at him. "Although, there do seem to be a few misconceptions you'll need to clear up."

Julian nodded, not surprised his master had heard their conversation. He'd left the door open, after all. "We have plenty of time for explanations."

After all, flying from Las Vegas to Paris wasn't a short trip.

"That you do." Jean-Paul patted him on the shoulder before moving away. "Holler if you need anything."

"Thank you, Jean-Paul," Julian responded heartfeltly before returning to finding his beloved sustenance.

Chapter Four

Waiting for Julian to return, Teason wondered how his life had suddenly taken a hard ninety-degree turn. It wasn't the first time, but he sure hoped it would be the last. His life had already been turned upside down once when his mother had met Rizzo, the lion shifter.

Not that I knew he was a lion shifter at the time.

Teason saw Julian's shadow before the man appeared in the doorway. With his head turned to the left, his temple resting against the headboard to keep the pressure off the cut on the back of it, he stared at the big man from the corner of his eye. Teason couldn't help but appreciate what he saw.

Guessing Julian was six-foot-three or maybe four, the vampire had broad shoulders and a trim waist, accentuated by the polo shirt that clung to him. His dress slacks fitted his long legs to perfection. Even the cut of his thick black hair, the tips of the strands just brushing his ears, accentuated his hard masculine features.

Stunning male.

And he's claiming that he's mine.

Huh. Maybe I better confirm just how similar a vampire's beloved is to a shifter's mate.

"You doing okay, *ma adorée*?" Julian asked as he placed the many packages he'd balanced onto the nightstand. "It's fine if you need a nap. Just try to eat a little first, please."

"I'm okay," Teason claimed, even though he realized his body had been threatening to drift off on him. *Must be the head wound.* Straightening, Teason asked, "Watcha got there?"

"I have sandwiches. Turkey or roast beef," Julian told him, holding one up in each hand. "Preference?" Then he quickly added, "If you don't mind me eating with you."

"Vampires eat real food?" Teason blurted the words in surprise. Feeling his cheeks heat, he mumbled, "Turkey, please."

Julian chuckled softly as he held out a turkey sub sandwich around four inches in length, wrapped in cellophane. "Yes," he confirmed, sitting on the bed facing him. He had one knee cocked out, and he left the other foot on the floor. "Vampires have to eat real food along with blood in order to sustain our health." As Julian began unwrapping his own sandwich, he commented, "Those shifters either didn't know much about us, or they didn't bother sharing it with you, did they?"

"I found out by accident," Teason admitted, unwrapping his own food. *Did I already tell him that?* Teason couldn't remember. Two packets fell from between the wrappings—mayo and mustard. "Um, so, you eat food. And you flew out during the day, so I guess that whole only awake at night thing is out the window, too." Setting aside the mustard, Teason opened the mayo packet and opened the sandwich so he could squirt it all over the top. "Oh, this sub bread is soft."

Inside the sub was not only the standard turkey and cheese that one would find at a truck stop, but there was lettuce, tomatoes, and pickles.

Yum!

Teason's stomach grumbled again.

"Most things movies make up about vampires are ridiculous," Julian told him as he doctored his own sandwich with mayo and mustard. "Holy water or other religious artifacts don't bother us. I personally find some of the churches in Montpellier absolutely stunning and their courtyards relaxing to sit in while eating gelato."

"Really?" Closing his sub back up, Teason lifted it to his lips. Before taking a bite, he asked, "Do vampires have a religion?"

"Um, not in the sense you're thinking of," Julian told him. He leaned over, grabbed three single-serving bags, and placed them on the bed between them. "Chili-flavored corn chips, French onion chips, and peanut-butter-filled pretzels."

Teason felt his brows lift as he took in the variety. He couldn't remember the last time he'd had any of them. Even as Teason chewed the delicious bite of his sandwich, he couldn't wait to open and try each of them.

"And just to make it seem like we're eating healthy." Julian winked as he tossed another couple of bags onto the comforter. "Dried apples and banana crisps."

Chuckling around his mouthful of food, Teason shook his head. "Do you guys eat like this all the time?" he asked once he'd swallowed. Then because the mini-sub tasted so good, Teason took another big bite. As he chewed that one, he carefully placed his sandwich on the cellophane before grabbing the bag of corn chips.

"Definitely not," Julian replied with a chuckle. "But even if we did, with a paranormal's higher metabolism, we'd process it just fine."

"Lucky you guys," Teason muttered before popping a corn chip into his mouth.

Julian reached out and touched Teason's knee. "Once we bond, your metabolism will speed up, too."

Teason's food nearly went down the wrong way as he choked a little. Coughing, he managed to unblock his airways and swallow his food. After grabbing the water bottle Julian had left him, Teason took a couple of quick gulps.

Once Teason had caught his breath, he squeaked, "Really?"

Nodding once, Julian sighed. "The shifters really didn't tell you much, huh?"

Before taking another drink, Teason shook his head.

"Okay, so . . ." Julian drew the word out as he opened all

the other bags, giving them both access. "Paranormal matings, bondings, whatever the species wants to call it, one-oh-one."

Teason nodded as he helped himself to a dried apple slice before picking up his sandwich again.

Julian smiled and began explaining between his own bites of food. "You asked if we were religious, and I said not really. We do however believe in Fate. The Moirai. The three fates. While we believe they weave the fabric of our lives, we still have free will." Even as Teason nodded, trying to understand, Julian held his gaze. "Paranormals live a long time. Centuries. Some species even longer."

"How old are you?" Teason blurted before shoving more food into his mouth just to keep himself from interrupting again.

Really? The Moirai?

If he recalled correctly from something he'd read long ago, they were supposed to be part of the Greek religion.

And he says they're not religious.

"I'm two-hundred-eighty-seven," Julian told him with an eyebrow waggle. "Look pretty good for an old guy, right?"

Teason barked a laugh, having been thinking the same thing. "Yeah."

"So, anyway," Julian continued. "Once a paranormal reaches their prime, normally in their early thirties, their body's aging slows to a snail's pace, and we'll look damn near the same for centuries."

That made sense, considering Rizzo and his mother looked about the same since the day his mom had brought him home.

"Due to this, we're a very insular community, keeping to ourselves, hiding in plain sight," Julian explained. "Vampires will often change covens every few decades or stop going out into public for a few years, then remake our identity as the son or daughter of whoever our last identity was."

Nodding again, Teason finished his sandwich, licking his

fingers.

Julian paused and stared, his nostrils flaring and his jaw clenching. For just a second, Teason thought the man's eyes turned red. Then it was gone, and the man seemed to shake himself and continue.

"Paranormals are stronger, faster, and have better senses than humans, but we don't breed as quickly as humans, which may explain the longer lifespan." Holding Teason's gaze, Julian told him, "Once we meet our fated beloved and bond with him or her, those attributes are passed to you to some degree."

"To some degree?" Teason took a few French onion chips before placing the bag back on the bed. "How so?"

"You won't be as strong or as fast as a vampire, but you'll notice a difference," Julian told him. "Also, you won't get sick or injured as easily. Your senses will improve." After a second of hesitation, Julian softly stated, "And your life thread will be tied to mine, so you'll live as long as I do . . . or die if I die."

"Oh," Teason whispered, his gut turning just a little. "G-Guess you guys take that whole 'til death do us part thing pretty seriously."

"We do," Julian confirmed quietly. "But on the flip side, I will be completely devoted to you. I will never raise my hand against you, and I'll never purposely say something to hurt you." Grimacing, Julian shrugged and added, "Although, I'm not perfect, and I've never been in a relationship, so I ask for forgiveness if I make a misstep here or there."

"Hey, no one's perfect," Teason murmured, his brain sorting through everything. "No relationship in nearly three centuries. Wow."

Julian shrugged. "I was waiting for my beloved."

"Sounds lonely." The words were out of Teason's mouth before he could censor them.

Scoffing softly, Julian tipped his chin in the smallest of

nods. "Yes. That's why paranormals consider mates and beloveds so highly." His voice remained soft, earnest, as he told him, "While some will pair with others for offspring, few form any permanent attachments, knowing that Fate could bring them their match at any moment."

"And I'm yours?"

Nodding again, Julian told him, "Yes." He reached over and took Teason's hand. "You are the other half of my soul. The person I've been searching for centuries for." After a second of hesitation as well as a squeeze of his hand, Julian told him, "And nothing would please me more than to bond us and share my life with you."

Teason's heart thudded in his chest as he stared at where Julian touched him. The hairs on his arm stood on end. Even his skin sort of tingled.

"N-Now I know why Mom moved Rizzo in so fast," Teason mused, trying to process his body's reactions. Rubbing his thumb over the back of Julian's hand, he asked, "Am I attracted to you just because your Fates say we should be together?"

"No." Julian shook his head. "We would have been attracted to each other anyway." Teason knew he hadn't kept the questioning look off his face when Julian explained, "The Fates just ramp up our attraction a bit, and they give the paranormal in the pairing the ability to recognize that the person is the other half of their soul." Julian opened his mouth again, hesitated, closing it. Then he blew out a breath and told him, "Either one of us could say no and walk away, but I'm praying to any gods that care to listen that won't be your response."

"I won't do that to you. I won't walk away," Teason murmured. Seeing Julian's eyes widen a smidge, he knew he needed to explain. "I've seen first-hand the way a paranormal will treat their mate, and I admit I'd love to have that for myself."

"You have?" Julian then nodded sharply. "Right. Your mother mated with a lion shifter." Cocking his head, he hesitantly asked, "May I ask how long ago that was?"

Teason tried to decide how much to share. The way his body was responding to the vampire was making continuing to think difficult. Especially since he was no longer filling the hole in his belly.

"Um, my dad died when I was eight. It was just me and my mom for years," Teason explained slowly, holding Julian's earnest gaze. "She rarely dated until Rizzo came along. That was when I was fourteen." Hesitating, Teason told him, "Rizzo moved in. I was a shit to him for at least six months, but he was patient with me. Finally, I acknowledged how happy he made my mother." With a sigh, he licked his lips. "When I was sixteen, my mom got pregnant." Teason grimaced and peered at the wall over Julian's shoulder. "They went to live with the pride, but said I couldn't come. They made up some bullshit excuse at the time, and they set me up with a one-bedroom apartment over the garage of one of our neighbors. That way, I wouldn't have to change schools."

"Holy shit," Julian growled, frowning. "Asshole."

Shrugging, Teason did his best to banish the loneliness his mother's apparent abandonment had caused. "They provided for me. I always had food, clothes, and a roof over my head. Money in my pocket. I just couldn't live with them."

"Our coven would have taken you into the secret," Julian declared, obviously upset on his behalf.

Teason felt his chest warm. "Yeah, well. They'd asked the alpha for permission, but he'd said no." Meeting Julian's fierce gaze caused a shiver of awareness to course through him. "Anyway, I found out when my loneliness and anger got the best of me. I went to their place unannounced and saw a couple of lions shift." Barking a laugh, Teason shook his head. "Suffice it to say, the alpha was pissed, the bare minimum was explained to me, and I was sworn to secrecy."

Teason knew that he'd even had a couple of shifters keeping an eye on him for at least a year before they decided to trust him.

Holding Julian's gaze, Teason explained, "So yeah, I understand the devotion, and . . ." Girding up his courage, he finished his thought. "And I would love to have someone of my own so damn bad."

Obviously understanding, Julian squeezed his hand and whispered huskily, "I will banish the loneliness from your soul, *ma adorée*."

"I'd like that," Teason murmured as he began watching Julian begin collecting the remnants of their meal. Surprisingly, there wasn't much. Just as the vampire began reaching for him once more, Teason cocked his head and frowned. "Wait."

Julian immediately froze, a question in his dark eyes.

Teason felt a wash of disappointment flood him as he asked, "I don't have my passport. How am I going to get into France?"

Chapter Five

Julian's tension melted away, and he chuckled upon hearing that *that* was his beloved's worry.

The sadness Julian had read in Teason's gorgeous hazel eyes made sense. While his mother and step-father had set his human up nicely, he'd essentially been abandoned. Julian couldn't fathom how someone could do that to a child.

Damn alpha and his unreasonable demands.

"Don't worry, Teason," Julian rumbled as he eased from the side of the bed. "You asked about being under a thrall, and I said we call our mental abilities trancing." Gripping the base of his polo, Julian whipped it over his head. "Remember?"

"Yeah."

Teason's response was breathy, and Julian loved the way his human's focus remained riveted on his chest.

"Well," Julian continued to explain, tossing the shirt on the floor as there wasn't anywhere else to place it in the plane's small bedroom. "We're landing at a private landing strip. If anyone asks questions, either myself or Jean-Paul will trance them, making them think they've already seen your passport."

"Oh."

As Julian had spoken, he'd unbuttoned and unzipped his fly, revealing his black boxer-briefs. Teason stared, his gleaming lips parted. His nostrils were flared, and his chest rose and fell in quick panting breaths.

"May I remove my clothes and join you on the bed, *ma adorée*?" Julian rumbled huskily. Realizing he really should have asked permission for what he hoped would come next, he quickly added, "May I remove your clothes and make love to your body, bonding us for eternity?"

"Eternity?"

The fact that Julian had rendered Teason to one-word answers was one hell of a stroke to his ego.

Grinning, Julian toed off his shoes and socks. "Well, our belief is that when a Fate-bonded pair dies, our souls will be reincarnated near each other, so we can find each other and bond again." While Julian had no idea if that was actually true, he'd always loved the romantic notion.

"Wow."

Yep. One-word answers. Just not the one I want to hear.

"Well, Teason?" Julian couldn't help the slight growl that filled his voice as he reveled in the way his—hopefully—soon-to-be lover was staring at him as he dropped his pants. His beloved's appreciation gleamed in his eyes, and Julian loved it, intending to see that look often. "May I join you?"

"Yes."

Finally.

Reaching over, Julian grabbed the lube from the nightstand.

Yep. Call me a fucking optimist.

"Thank you, *ma adorée*," Julian muttered as he climbed onto the bed. He'd removed Teason's shoes and safety vest after bandaging his head. "I will take such good care of you."

Reaching for Teason's foot, Julian first removed one sock, then the other, taking a moment to massage his human's arches. He grinned upon hearing his beloved's groan of appreciation. The sound ramped up his desire, slamming him with a surge of lust.

"Gods, I do love the sounds you make," Julian muttered, reaching up to grip the hem of his beloved's polo shirt. "Lift your arms," he encouraged. Even as Teason seemed to eagerly obey, Julian warned, "We must be careful of your head."

Gently, Julian eased the light fabric over Teason's head. The garment joined the rest of the clothes on the floor. Seeing his human propped up on his elbows so the back of his head didn't touch the pillow, Julian took a few seconds to admire his lean frame. His skin was naturally pale, and his freckles went all the way down, drawing a moan from Julian. Teason's narrow torso rose and fell in swift breaths, and a flush of arousal almost caused his skin to glow.

"One day soon," Julian claimed, reaching for Teason's fly. "I'm going to nibble and count each and every one of your freckles."

"Y-You don't mind them?"

Hearing the worry in Teason's tone, Julian glanced up from where he unzipped his cargo shorts. He spotted the way his human nibbled his bottom lip. Teason's expression clearly betrayed his uncertainty, and that just wouldn't do.

"I *love* them," Julian declared as he undid Teason's fly. "They're part of you."

Not wanting to give Teason a chance to second-guess him, Julian leaned over and licked over a freckle on his left ribcage. He grinned when he heard his human's gasp. As Julian began tracking licks, nips, and kisses over the dots on his soft stomach, he eased the shorts down Teason's thighs.

Julian leaned up so he could pull the fabric free, leaving Teason in a pair of dark gray briefs. His human's erection was clearly outlined within the confining fabric. Unable to help himself, Julian cupped his beloved's length.

Teason moaned and bucked, his back arching.

Unfortunately, the move also caused the back of his head to touch the pillow beneath him. His lover froze and hissed for a different reason.

"Easy, Teason," Julian murmured, releasing his cock in favor of rubbing a soothing hand up his side. He kept his weight on his other hand as he levered over his beloved. Touching his jaw to gain his attention, Julian peered into his eyes, a mixture of pleasure and pain swirling within the depths of his hazel gaze. "As much as I want to take you face to face, so I can make love to your mouth with my tongue, that will have to wait until I've healed the wound on the back of your head."

"Y-You can do that?" When Julian nodded, Teason asked, "How?"

"My saliva," Julian explained. Spotting Teason's clearly confused frown, he told him, "It's how a vampire heals the mark of his bite after feeding from a donor." *Or unknowing human.* "My saliva will heal the wound."

Without missing a beat, Teason guessed, "So, you could heal the cut on the back of my head simply by licking it?"

"I can," Julian assured. While that wasn't a traditional use of a vampire's saliva, he knew it could work. "If you're okay with it, I'll put you on your knees, and while I play with your pretty ass and open you up for my cock, I will heal your head." At the mental image he was painting in his head, Julian couldn't help but growl as his cock twitched within the confines of his underwear. "Then I will slide into you, fuck you, and claim you as mine."

Groaning, his nostrils flaring, Teason gasped, "Yes. Oh, god, yes."

Grinning broadly, anticipation causing his blood to burn, Julian knew Teason had spotted his fangs when he inhaled sharply.

Teason eased onto one elbow so he could reach up and touch the corner of Julian's mouth with the other. "To claim me, you'll have to bite me?"

Flicking out his tongue, Julian licked the pad of Teason's finger. He tasted hints of his beloved's flavor as well as a trace of salt from the chips he'd been eating. Humming, Julian did it again, enjoying every aspect of being with his human.

"Yes, I will bite you," Julian responded when he remembered that Teason had asked a question. Seeing the concern in his expressive eyes, he assured, "And you will come from it."

Gaping, Teason stared at him in obvious shock. "No way."

Julian nodded. "Yes way."

Swooping down, Julian pecked a hard kiss to Teason's mouth. He quickly pulled back, not wanting to possibly injure his human further. Instead, Julian quickly helped Teason shuck his underwear before doing the same with his own.

Upon seeing Teason lick his lips—his human's gaze riveted to Julian's throbbing cock—he groaned and shook his head. "Gods, I want to feel your lips on me so badly, *ma adorée*," he admitted, reading the desire in Teason's eyes. "But another time."

Without waiting for a response, Julian gripped Teason's hips. He helped his beloved turn onto his front. Upon seeing the gorgeous mounds of his human's bubble butt, Julian growled with delight. He even had to grip the base of his prick with one hand to stem his sudden desire to spray his seed all over the beautiful flesh laid out before him.

Gods. This is going to be embarrassing. I'm going to come so fucking fast.

Caressing one of Teason's ass cheeks, Julian grabbed the lube with the other. He knew he needed to get the show on the road or there wouldn't be a show. Hearing Teason's whimper and feeling the way his human arched into his touch didn't really help.

"Easy, *ma adorée*," Julian purred, pulling his hand away. "Gods, you're so sensual." He popped the cap and poured lube onto his fingers. "So responsive."

"Please, Julian," Teason murmured, peering over his shoulder at him. "I need."

"I know what you need, Teason," Julian assured, setting

the tube aside. "Let me take care of you. I wish to make you feel so good." With his clean hand, Julian reached for the bandage. "I'm sorry about the pain from it sticking to your hair a bit."

"It's fine." With a wry smile twisting his lips as he looked back at him, Teason told him, "It'll help me calm down so I don't embarrass myself."

Julian chuckled even as he began working the bandage off of Teason's head. Hearing his beloved's hiss and seeing his occasional wince, he decided it would do the exact same thing for him, too. Julian hated that he was hurting his beloved, even in such a small way.

Finally, Julian got it removed. He folded it in on itself before tossing it to the floor. It occurred to him that he would have a hell of a lot to clean up later. Just as quickly, he dismissed the thought to move on to the matter at hand.

"On your elbows, Teason," Julian encouraged, rubbing his hand up and down the back of his neck. "And just relax for me. This may feel a little weird."

"Okay."

Julian's heart raced as Teason immediately did as he was told. The amount of faith his beloved was displaying caused a bloom of something other than arousal within him. He knew it was far too soon for love, but as a paranormal, Julian knew he was well on his way.

My beloved. All mine.

With those thoughts swirling through his mind, Julian levered over Teason fully. He felt his cock slip between his human's thighs, and he gritted his teeth against the pleasant tingles it caused within his balls. Calling upon his centuries of experience and control, Julian pushed thoughts of his need from his mind and lowered his lips to Teason's head.

After nuzzling through Teason's hair, enjoying the rich aroma of his blood, Julian stuck out his tongue. The first lick yanked a soft moan from him. His blood tasted like the finest of ambrosia. Swiping his tongue gently along the damaged flesh over and over, for a moment, Julian lost himself to the simple pleasure of tasting his forever love.

Hearing Teason's soft moan pulled Julian out of his blood-drunk state. He remembered what else he was supposed to be doing. As he continued to clean the blood from between Teason's hairs and healing the wound, Julian eased his fingertips along the trench of his beloved's body.

With the skill of centuries of sex, Julian easily found his goal. He teased over his beloved's opening, relaxing the muscle. A few seconds later, Julian eased his first finger in, and the heat and squeeze ripped a groan from his throat.

"Oh, yeah," Teason whined, canting his hips, asking for more with his body. "Please, Julian," he pleaded. "It all feels so good."

Doing as his beloved bid, Julian picked up the pace. After all, he was right there with him in his need.

Gonna make him mine. My beloved. Ma adorée.

With that single thought rattling through his mind, Julian quickly added a second finger.

Chapter Six

When Julian had mentioned licking him, Teason had felt a smidge grossed out. Just as quickly, he'd recalled the man's fangs and the fact that he was a vampire. Julian would enjoy his blood any way that he could get it.

So Teason had pushed the oddness from his mind. Still, it had taken every bit of self-control he had to keep from tensing when Julian had begun to lick him. He thought it would hurt . . . a person sliding his tongue over the injured areas of his scalp.

Instead, the strangest thing had happened. The area had begun to . . . tingle. Each consecutive lick had felt better than the last, chasing away the pain in his head. The sensation of Julian's tongue had started to feel . . . fantastic, as if the vampire was licking other parts of his body.

Good god!

Teason moaned softly, and when Julian had paused, Teason hadn't been above begging. He wanted those odd sensations to continue . . . desperately. His entire body felt hot, shaky, burning with a need he couldn't seem to put into words. His erection throbbed in time with his heartbeat, and he'd barely resisted reaching for his prick. Only the fear that he would fall flat on his face had stayed the move.

Fortunately, Julian seemed to know exactly what he needed. The big vampire had eased a finger into Teason's chute, then another, opening him swiftly yet with care.

Unable to hold in his sounds, Teason moaned and whimpered. He twisted his fingers into the comforter, giving him a little leverage to rock into each of Julian's finger-thrusts. His chute felt full and empty at the same time, and all the while, Julian continued the weird onslaught to the nerve endings on his head.

Teason had never thought he'd had a licking fetish, but he could become addicted to Julian's tongue so damn fast.

"Please, Julian," Teason whined, the dual pleasure to his scalp and channel causing his body to rack with sensations his brain couldn't process. All Teason knew was that he never wanted it to end, and yet, he needed it to all the same. Teason needed . . ."More," he pleaded. "Please, more."

"You'll have me, *ma adorée,*" Julian growled into his ear, his voice deep and rough. "You'll have me."

"Now," Teason urged. "Please now."

"Yessss," Julian hissed, easing his fingers from Teason's body. "Now, *ma adorée.*"

Each time Julian used his pet name, Teason felt as if his heart skipped a beat in his chest. His shiver worked down his spine. He couldn't believe how much he enjoyed the clear possessiveness in those simple words.

This is my vampire. He wants me . . . forever. I'll never be alone again.

Teason felt the broad head of the thick cock kiss his hole. He knew Julian sported a very impressive erection. He'd seen it before the vampire had urged him to roll over.

Even though Teason had never taken a cock so large, his body seemed to crave it. When the vampire pushed, his muscles gave way easily. He barely had to push out before his new lover's mushroom cap slipped inside his body, stretching him wide.

Groaning, Teason relished the ever-so-slight burn of the stretch. Perhaps misunderstanding, Julian froze.

No!

Not liking that, Teason let out a quiet growl. He arched his back just a little more. Using his hold on the comforter, he pushed backward, managing to impale himself just a bit more on Julian's cock.

"Ah, *ma adorée*," Julian groaned, slipping into his natural language. "Stay still. I don't want to hurt you."

"You won't," Teason assured in English, revealing he understood. "Need to feel all of you."

"My sexy, intelligent beloved," Julian rumbled into his ear even as he started moving once more. "Love that you understand me."

Teason moaned as he felt Julian push in and in and in. "Un-Underst-stand," he stuttered. Then the vampire's thick shaft slid over his prostate, and he finished on a moan.

"Sexy sounds," Julian damn near snarled into his ear. "Love them." He paused with his thighs pressed flush to Teason's own, but only for an instant. "Want more."

Then Julian pulled nearly all the way out before slamming back in.

"Yesssss," Teason hissed, reveling in the power behind Julian's ruts. The vampire hit Teason's prostate with nearly every stroke, and he couldn't have stopped the whimpers and moans erupting from his throat even if his life had depended on it. Every move Julian made felt better than anything Teason had ever before experienced, and his balls quickly tightened.

When Julian pressed his lips to the back of his head and swiped out his tongue once more, Teason lost it. Without a touch, his erection throbbed, his balls forcing spurt after spurt of seed from within him. His gut clenched, as did his chute, with the force of the orgasm roaring through his veins.

Teason opened his mouth on a silent scream as his body shuddered and jolted. He barely felt it when Julian's teeth pierced the flesh where his neck met his shoulder. A second later, when the vampire began to suck the life blood from his veins, *that* he felt.

Bliss-inducing zings washed over Teason's flesh. His nipples tingled, and his flesh goose bumped. He sucked in a shocked gasp as the sensations went straight to his groin. Teason felt his cock swell as his balls pulled tight once more.

Black spots danced across Teason's vision as a second orgasm, nearly as powerful as the first, crashed over him, pulling him under like a riptide.

The gentle stroking of a hand down his spine registered to Teason first. The next thing he noticed with the warm flesh under his cheek. Finally, Teason realized his torso rose and fell with the rate of each exhaled breath that fanned over the top of his head.

"You back with me, *ma adorée*?" Julian murmured, teasing his fingers along his scalp. "Was beginning to worry."

Teason smiled. "My vampire," he whispered, flexing his fingers, feeling firm, warm flesh beneath his palm, and he realized he was cradling the man's ribcage. "Is this real?"

"*Oui*, Teason," Julian confirmed before nuzzling his lips against his hair. "This is real." Sliding a couple of fingers under Teason's jaw, Julian urged him to look up at him. When Teason obeyed, he saw an expression on the vampire's face that could almost be called loving. Julian smiled, his expression relaxed, his dark eyes full of warmth. "I, too, can hardly believe it. You've made me the happiest vampire in the world."

Feeling something in the vicinity of his heart flutter, Teason softly replied, "Me, too." He felt his cheeks heat a bit even as he saw Julian's grin, his pointy fangs on clear display, as he amended, "Human. Uh, happiest human."

"Good." Lifting his head, Julian pecked a quick kiss to his lips before relaxing his head on the pillow again. "I'm very happy to hear that."

For a moment, they continued to gaze at each other, and

Teason wondered what Julian could possibly be thinking.

Do you have any questions for me, ma adorée*?*

Jolting, Teason lifted his head and stared at Julian.

The vampire just winked.

"D-Did I—" Teason began to stutter. "D-Did you—"

Teason wasn't certain how to finish his question without sounding like a total loon.

Oui, *you did hear my voice in your head.* Oui, *I am speaking to you telepathically.*

Opening his mouth, Julian spoke out loud. "My apologies, Teason. I didn't mean to startle you." His tone turned a little rueful. "I forgot that shifters do not have that capability with their fated mate."

"You can speak to me telepathically?" Teason asked for want of anything else.

"I can," Julian confirmed.

"Can you read my mind?" Teason's brain immediately jumped to the next conclusion.

"No, I cannot read your mind," Julian assured with a smile. "Just like you cannot read my mind. Although, you can project your thoughts to me telepathically, just like I can with you."

Teason nodded slowly. Settling back down, he rested his chin on his hand on the side of Julian's chest. "Is this something all vampires share?" After a quick glance toward the front of the plane, Teason wondered, "Like, can you speak with your vampire buddies out there in your heads?"

Shaking his head, Julian told him, "No, sharing a telepathic link is only between bonded beloveds. Special to the pair." He lifted a hand and pointed it toward the front of the plane before returning it to Teason's back and starting to trace over his spine again. "And that does remind me that there are a few other things we need to discuss."

"Okay." Teason sort of already felt on information overload, but he resisted saying that to his vampire lover. "Like what?"

"I only have one vampire buddy out there." Julian's lips quirked up as if he found the words amusing. "Out there is Master Jean-Paul Tremblay, leader of our vampire coven."

"Leader?" Teason whispered, racking his brain, trying to remember if he'd done anything that might have offended him. Except, he couldn't recall actually meeting him. "Um, is there, uh, like, protocol when you introduce me? Do I need to bow or kneel or something?"

"No, *ma adorée*," Julian replied with a chuckle, clearly finding the question amusing. "However, when we are with others, never contradict him or question his orders." Teasing his fingers through the hair at Teason's nape, Julian continued, "Doing so in private is allowed when done respectfully, but he is the master. His word is the final say."

Blowing out a breath, Teason nodded once. "Kinda like how that lion alpha told my mom that she couldn't tell me about shifters," he muttered, feeling a little unsettled by that. "And that I couldn't live on pride lands with them when she got pregnant with a shifter baby."

"I am so sorry for that, Teason," Julian quickly told him. "While part of me understands his reasoning, that secrecy is the number one rule for all paranormals' safety, most alphas in his situation would have made an exception." With a growl, Julian added, "That alpha sounds like an asshole." Julian scowled. "And your mother's mate should have gotten you permission years before when you were younger. That way, you would have been indoctrinated into the shifter culture, so you'd already have understood the need for secrecy." As if somehow reading Teason's unease, Julian tacked on, "It's what Jean-Paul would have done. He never would have separated a parent from their underage child. Not ever."

Julian sounded so certain that Teason believed him.

"Okay." Teason left it at that. Changing the subject, because dwelling on the past did no one any good, he mentioned, "I heard two voices out there. Uh, Saul, I think was the other one."

"Indeed. Saul Mandisa is Jean-Paul's beloved, just as you are mine." Chuckling softly, Julian told him, "Saul is also human." He continued to grin as he mused, "What are the odds that both the coven master and the head enforcer both found their fated beloved on a trip to Las Vegas?"

Scoffing, Teason murmured, "Yeah, what are the odds." Realizing what else Julian had said, he popped his head up again. "Wait. Did you just say you're the head enforcer?"

Julian grinned broadly. "Indeed, I am."

Wow. Sexy and powerful. Boy, did I luck out!

Chapter Seven

"Damn, man. I can't believe I'm walking around Paris." Saul grinned broadly, his thick blond hair gleaming in the sun. Nudging Teason's upper arm, he asked, "Can you, Tea?"

Julian watched, smiling, pleasure thrumming through him as Teason grinned back at the much larger human.

"Never thought I'd ever get to come here," Teason admitted. He stared around in wonder, turning this way and that as if he worried he would miss something. "This is so gorgeous!"

Slipping his arm around Teason's waist, Julian murmured, "Wait until we take you up the Eiffel Tower this evening." He enjoyed the look of shock on his beloved's face when he focused up at him. "The lights of the city will amaze you."

"Really?" Teason grinned broadly at him. "That'll be so awesome."

Teason lifted on his toes and pecked a kiss to his lips. Just as quickly, he continued walking, his expression turning shy . . . then apprehensive. The way Teason glanced around made Julian realize why.

They were in public.

"No one around here cares about such displays between men," Julian assured, whispering the words in Teason's ear. He squeezed his beloved human's hip and used his chin to indicate to the right. "See?"

A pair of men were sitting in front of a bistro. Their chairs were close together, and they were sharing a plate of beignets.

Considering the way they were feeding each other the powdered pastries, anyone could see they were a couple.

No one around frowned at them, glared, or even paid them much mind.

"Huh," Teason murmured.

Julian had learned over the flight that Teason would say that when he really didn't have anything else to say. From the time they'd exited the flight at the private airstrip, to the limo to their Paris hotel, to their exploration of their two-bedroom suite, and even throughout their walk, Julian's poor beloved had been saying that a lot. Julian realized that his sweet human hadn't gotten out much.

When Julian had asked about that—after all, he'd been working at an airport—Teason had admitted that he'd never once used the perks to fly anywhere. He didn't have too much extra after living expenses. With the way his mother and stepfather had left him on his own, once Teason had graduated from high school, he had wanted to rely only on himself.

As gently as Julian could, he'd reminded Teason that he wasn't alone anymore. The gorgeous smile that Julian had received from his beloved had damn near caused his heart to stop. Only the fact that they had dinner reservations had stopped Julian from ravaging Teason in their hotel room.

As it was, that hadn't stopped Julian from enjoying a very wonderful frotting session with his beloved in the shower.

Gods, I love the way his wet slippery body feels rubbing against mine.

Just thinking about it had a predictable reaction on Julian's body, and he felt his prick plumping in his slacks.

Jean-Paul met Julian's gaze and gave him a knowing smirk, probably having scented his sudden surge of arousal.

"So, where are we headed?" Saul asked curiously. His head was on a swivel, too, glancing this way and that. "Do we have time to check out the Louvre?"

Julian had been surprised to discover that Jean-Paul's massive blond beloved enjoyed art and museums. When they'd told their humans that they were stopping in Paris for a few days—since neither of them had ever even been out of Nevada—both men had expressed their excitement. While Teason had a list of landmarks he wanted to see, Saul had wanted to check out a couple of museums.

"Of course, my beloved," Jean-Paul answered as he gazed up at his slightly taller human. "We'll head over there first thing tomorrow morning."

"Sweet," Saul responded affably.

When Jean-Paul had discovered that Saul was his beloved, Julian had wondered if his coven master would have a problem with the fact that Saul was actually larger than himself. While Jean-Paul stood six-foot-three with a toned, muscular frame, Saul stood six-foot-five. The human also sported a bulky frame with thick muscles.

Julian had discreetly asked about the bedroom situation, and Jean-Paul had offered him a toothy grin while saying, "For the most part, my beloved is an amazing power bottom."

Dropping it, Julian had read between the lines. On occasion, his coven master bottomed for his human. Julian never would have guessed it, but as any paranormal, he bet that his master wanted his beloved happy.

"Ah, here we are." Jean-Paul indicated the restaurant to their left. "I absolutely love the escargot here."

Humming appreciatively, Julian nodded and began guiding Teason that way.

Saul scoffed as he followed Jean-Paul's lead, the pair holding hands. "Can't say as I've ever had snails." He shrugged his massive shoulders and quipped, "But as they say, when in Rome."

"We're not in Rome, baby," Jean-Paul teased right back.

Grinning, Saul just shrugged again.

Stepping forward, Julian opened the door. He had just a second of indecision, pausing with the door half open. While he wanted to protect his beloved—and his coven master—and go first so he could check the room for danger, Julian also knew it was good manners to allow his date to precede him.

"Relax, Julian," Jean-Paul murmured. "We have your back. All will be fine."

Blowing out a harsh breath, Julian cast a wry smile his master's way. Then he finished opening the door, allowing Teason to go first. Saul grabbed the door from his hand and offered a wide grin.

Julian just bet that Jean-Paul had used their telepathic link to share his dilemma with him. So far, Teason had only used it a couple of times when Julian had encouraged him. Julian hoped his human would grow more comfortable with it before too long.

"Good evening, gentlemen," the host greeted in French. "Four this evening?" He was already gathering the menus.

"I have a reservation," Jean-Paul told him, answering in the same language. Saul didn't seem to mind, peering around the dining establishment with interest. "Under Jean-Paul Tremblay."

"Ah, Mister Tremblay. Good evening." The man obviously recognized Tremblay's name, as he was listed as the owner of the large vineyard in Montpellier. "A pleasure having you with us this evening." Taking a step backward, the host indicated to the right. "Please come with me. We have a secluded table set up in the back."

"Thank you," Jean-Paul responded, starting to follow him and taking Saul with him.

Resting his hand on Teason's lower back, Julian kept his beloved close. He followed even as he glanced discreetly around the room. It wasn't a surprise that he could make out the smells of both shifters and vampires amidst the humans.

After all, Paris was a popular vacation and tourist location for, well . . . everyone.

"Here you are, sirs." The host began placing the menus around the bench seat of a lavish booth that could have sat six people easily. "Monique will be your server this evening." With a wide smile, he focused on Jean-Paul. "Being a wine connoisseur of your caliber, would you like me to pass on a request from you, sir?"

"Thank you for the compliment," Jean-Paul told him with a small smile. "I believe I'll wait until my partner has decided on his meal."

Dipping his head in deference, the host stated, "Of course, sir. Please, enjoy your meal."

After the host had hurried away, Saul rested his forearms on the table as he smirked at Jean-Paul. "You know I didn't understand much of that." He kept his voice low. "But that guy was seriously kissing your ass." Quirking a blond brow, Saul asked, "You known around these parts?"

Jean-Paul chuckled as he picked up Saul's hand with his own and brought it to his lips. "Our coven's vineyard"—he kept his voice low—"has a reputation in the wine industry." Then he pressed a kiss to Saul's palm even as he gave his beloved a heated look.

"Ooooh." Saul nodded in understanding. "That why I met you in a wine bar?"

With a laugh, Jean-Paul shook his head. "No, that location was chosen by our friends."

"Well, I'm glad they did," Saul rumbled back, his happiness clear.

I feel like I'm intruding on a private moment.

Julian nearly jolted upon hearing Teason's voice in his head. Pleased his beloved had initiated the contact, he wrapped his arm along the back of the booth. As Julian rubbed Teason's neck, he responded.

Even though they have been together for nearly three weeks, I'd still call them in the honeymoon phase. But, yes, sometimes watching them can give me a sweet tooth.

Think we'll ever be that comfortable together?

Julian didn't miss the wistfulness in Teason's mental voice.

Dismissing the menu, Julian turned his focus on Teason. His beloved was staring at the menu, but there was a slightly vacant look that made Julian think his human wasn't really seeing it.

Gently, Julian reached over with his free hand and cradled Teason's jaw. He felt, heard, and saw his beloved's gasp as he turned to look at him. Julian smiled, finding the shy look on his beloved's face oddly arousing.

We have just met. Leaning toward Teason, Julian continued to hold his human's gaze. *We are still learning about each other.* Unable to help himself, Julian pressed a gentle butterfly kiss to Teason's full lips. Upon pulling away, he saw the dazed look of wonder filling his human's eyes. *We'll get there,* ma adorée. *I promise you. It will just take time.* Then Julian winked as he allowed his gaze to turn heated. *And just so you know, I would welcome your touch and kiss anytime, anywhere.*

Really?

Yes, Julian definitely heard the awe in Teason's tone.

Really.

Just as Julian sent that mental confirmation, he heard Jean-Paul clear his throat. He glanced his coven master's way and noticed their server had arrived. Even spotting the tell-tale blush working up his beloved's freckled cheeks, Julian refused to show any embarrassment at being caught in their private moment.

Instead, Julian glanced at the menu's appetizers before telling the smiling woman and ordering a bottle of wine he knew they carried that he liked. "Also, please start an order of the smoked salmon canapes."

Monique smiled widely. "Of course, sir. I'll get those started and be back with your wine in a minute." Then she was gone.

"We almost ordered those." Jean-Paul switched to English, probably for his beloved's benefit. "We chose the escargot instead."

"Talked you into snails, did he?" Julian chuckled, grinning at Saul.

Saul grinned, showing off his even white teeth. "Like I said, when in Rome."

As Julian and his fellow vampire chuckled, Teason touched his arm, drawing his attention. "Would it be rude to ask to try one of their appetizers?"

Before Julian had a chance to answer, Saul chuckled and told him, "Not at all." Relaxing in his seat, he told him, "Besides, we ordered two platters, and I want to try your salmon canapes."

Jean-Paul smirked at Julian. "I knew you'd want some, too."

Nodding, Julian appreciated his friend's thoughtfulness. "You're not wrong."

Just then, Monique returned with their bottles of wine.

Julian recognized the label that Jean-Paul had chosen, appreciating his choice. Like him, he'd gone with something that could go with just about any meal they chose.

Uh, I can't read the menu. My French isn't that good.

Hearing Teason continuing to use their mind-link, Julian just managed to keep from preening.

Do you trust me?

Of course.

Loving his beloved's immediate response, Julian rested his hand on Teason's thigh and gave it a squeeze. At the same time, he swept his gaze over the menu. He'd had a chance to look at it on his phone while at their hotel room as they'd been waiting for the concierge to bring clothes for Teason, so he had a pretty good idea of his choices.

When Jean-Paul was done ordering for him and Saul, Julian took over for himself and Teason.

After getting a, "Very good, sirs," from Monique, she disappeared again.

As Julian watched Teason enjoy the wine he'd chosen, he was filled with a rush of contentment he'd never before experienced, but he never intended to be without it again.

Chapter Eight

Dinner had come with a few interesting revelations to Teason.

To his shock, he'd enjoyed the escargot.

No, not even that.

Teason had *loved* the escargot. When the two plates of appetizers were empty, Julian had noticed his looks of disappointment and longing. To his surprise, even though Teason had a perfectly lovely steak and lobster tail in front of him, along with a heap of wonderful mashed potatoes with just the right hints of garlic—the asparagus he could have done without—*Yuck*—Julian had ordered three more rounds of the escargot.

"Wait, I don't really need more," Teason had tried to object.

Julian had chuckled while waving away his complaint before confirming his request for three more plates of escargot.

When Teason had looked at Jean-Paul and Saul, the first had been smirking with obvious amusement while nodding, and the second had been grinning.

In that moment, Teason had a tough time remembering that Jean-Paul was a master vampire. He'd only met Rizzo's alpha once, and he'd been so much different—glowering, cold, and judgmental. Maybe that was the difference between a good leader and a bad one, or perhaps it was the difference between vampires and shifters.

Teason had no way of knowing.

Instead, Teason had just appreciated the additional opportunity to enjoy the slightly salty, weirdly textured tasty morsels.

When Monique had brought the additional appetizers to the table, she'd grinned broadly and asked if they needed anything else. There was a definite twinkle in her eye. Pleasure appeared to fill her dark orbs when both vampires had ordered a second bottle of wine.

Having never been much of a wine drinker before, Teason had taken it easy, even though whatever Julian had ordered had tasted fantastic. He'd always relied on himself once he realized what was going on with his mother—*at least she's happy now, although maybe I should call her*. Instead, Teason had focused on making his own way, so he hadn't indulged in activities that could get rather expensive—going out to eat, alcohol on a regular basis, or frivolous electronic extras that he just didn't understand.

A TV is a TV, right?

When Julian reached over and snagged his half-eaten steak from his plate, Teason was yanked from his weird thoughts. "Thank you," he whispered, even as he piled another three escargot onto his plate. "I would never have tried these before, but, shit, they're amazing!"

"I'm so very pleased to find someone who loves them as much as I do, Teason," Jean-Paul claimed, relaxing back in his seat. The vampire master had one arm around Saul, who was still slowly making his way through the last bits of his meal. "Now, when I ask the chef to make it, I won't feel like I'm asking him to cook just for me."

In that moment, Teason actually felt as if the master vampire was . . . well . . . approachable.

Just another regular guy. Someone with a handsome partner, looking for acceptance.

Teason could understand that.

Offering Jean-Paul a tentative smile, Teason offered, "If your chef makes them taste anything like this"—he used his petite fork to point at the shelled delicacy on his plate—"I will oh-so-happily eat them with you." With a laugh, Teason added, "In quantity."

Laughing, Jean-Paul stated, "As the Cajun say, we'll have a good ol' fashion crawfish boil."

"You like crawfish?" Saul stared at Jean-Paul in surprise, the last of his garlic mashed potatoes threatening to drop off his fork, which had paused between his plate and his mouth. "Really?"

"*Oui*, my beloved," Jean-Paul rumbled huskily, his attention zooming into narrow-focus on Saul. "I've been to the bayou a time or two."

Then the master lifted a hand to ease Saul's fork closer to his lips, and his lover dutifully ate his last bite. The move didn't hide the hunger in Saul's eyes, though.

Turning away from them, Teason focused on Julian. His vampire lover was flicking his gaze over his master, but quickly returned his attention to him. He smiled and winked, letting him know all was well.

"So do you want dessert, *ma adorée*?"

"How can you think of dessert when you stole my—Oh." Looking at Julian's plate, Teason realized his vampire lover had completely polished off the remains of his steak. He'd even eaten all the asparagus—*Yuck*. "At least you left me a couple of bites of lobster tail."

"Yes, I did," Julian replied in a husky tone. "How thoughtful of me."

With a snort, Teason felt his cheeks heat. He spotted Monique approaching out of the corner of his eye, so he fought back a snicker as he focused on finishing up his last couple of escargots—*so damn good, even though I'm stuffed*—and the last few bites of potatoes.

"Is there anything else I can get for you all, sirs?" Monique asked brightly. "Some boxes? Oh." She grinned even as the widening of her eyes betrayed her surprise.

Yeah. Paranormals can eat a lot.

"Would any of you care to see the dessert menu?" Monique switched gears.

"Not this time," Jean-Paul told her, even as he blatantly rubbed his thumb up and down the side of Saul's neck. "We need to get to the Eiffel Tower soon. The check, please?"

"Of course, sir." Monique pulled a billfold from a side pocket and placed it on the table. "I'll be back shortly."

"Wait." Jean-Paul's voice was low but firm. He picked up the billfold and opened it, saying, "We have an appointment soon." After slipping the ticket a little way out, obviously scanning it, he pulled out a black card. After tucking it into the folder, Jean-Paul handed it back to Monique. "Hurry, please."

"Right away, sir," Monique replied with an actual bow-like move. Then she scurried off.

Teason did his best to keep his breathing even. He'd seen the total. Considering he assumed it was in Euros, he knew that meant it was even more in US dollars.

Holy shit!

"While she's runnin' that, I'm gonna hit the head," Saul claimed. Making a shooing motion with his hands, he smiled at Jean-Paul. "Let me out, handsome."

For an instant, Jean-Paul looked like he wanted to disagree. With a sigh, he scooted from his side of the booth. "Stay in contact," he whispered, tapping his temple. "You remember what happened last time."

"I remember," Saul replied softly. While his eyes sparkled with mischief, he kept his tone even as he stated, "I'll keep you posted as I piss."

Jean-Paul scoffed and rolled his eyes.

Feeling the call of nature himself, Teason squeezed Julian's thigh. "You mind if I go, too?"

Julian froze only an instant before he moved, allowing Teason to rise from his side of the booth. "Stay in touch," his vampire urged before pecking a kiss to his lips.

Teason nodded. "Will do."

Then Teason hurried after Saul. The big blond glanced over his shoulder at him, a wry smile curving his lips, but he didn't say anything. At least, not until they were in the men's room.

Saul actually went so far as to check under the stall doors before heading to the urinal. Taking his cue from the man who'd known the vampires a bit longer than himself, Teason moved to another urinal. As he began unzipping, he noticed Saul peering slightly to the left as if he were eyeing the door.

"Don't judge them too harshly about security shit," Saul muttered even as the sound of his stream hitting the bowl filled the room. "They have reasons for it."

After letting out a breath, Teason felt his own bladder release, and he started to piss. "Yeah?" he asked. "What do you mean?"

Glancing his way, Saul revealed that a smirk curved his lips. "I mean, the last time I went to the bathroom in a restaurant by myself, some bad dudes kidnapped me." With a roll of his shoulders, he reached forward and flushed. "They're just cautious, is all."

Teason's stream dried up, his bladder empty, and he quickly flushed and zipped so he could follow Saul to the sinks. "Shit. They had enemies in Vegas that went after you?" Staring in the mirror at the larger man who was also washing his hands. "How'd you escape? Or did they rescue you?"

The guy looks so calm!

"Naw, those were *my* enemies," Saul admitted with a grimace. "But they did save me." After drying his hands, he peered at him with deep blue eyes. "All I'm sayin' is, you obey when they tell you to do somethin' that's in regards to your safety. All right? And never forget your bond." Saul tapped his temple.

Nodding quickly, Teason immediately agreed. "All right."

"Come on." Saul tapped the backs of his fingers against Teason's upper arm before leading the way out of the men's room.

Teason followed.

By the time they returned to the table, Monique must have returned Jean-Paul's card. Both men stood beside the table, quietly talking with each other. Teason's tension eased when they both smiled, Julian's attention fixated on him.

When Teason reached Julian's side, he immediately snuggled against the large vampire. He wrapped his arm around his lover's waist. Teason tipped his head back and accepted a kiss from the man.

In that moment, Teason realized he could truly get used to that sort of thing—never having to hide his feelings for another man. He hoped it would be just the same when they reached Montpellier. On the flight, Julian had told him about his coven home and how wonderful it was, and Teason desperately wanted it to be so.

"Are you ready for the Eiffel Tower?" Julian asked softly, turning Teason toward the exit.

"Absolutely." Teason could hardly wait.

Julian guided them out of the restaurant, turning left once they hit the street. They walked at a leisurely pace, but it was steady. His lover pointed out different shops and places he'd been to before, telling him about why they were memorable to him.

On the walk, Teason could hear Jean-Paul and Saul talking behind them, but he couldn't make out their soft murmurs. He felt as if he and Julian were alone, that it was just them on their date, even though, in his head, he knew it was an illusion. Still, that sense made Teason feel the date was special, and he relished every second of it.

They'd just turned the corner, the Eiffel Tower appearing

over the rooftops a few streets ahead, when three men separated from the shadows, standing in their path.

To Teason's surprise, they each carried a sword. The metal gleamed in the street lights.

"Come with us peacefully," the guy standing in the middle demanded, his chin jutting toward the alley they'd just left. A definite snarl entered his tone as he continued, "Or your little humans will die."

Even as fear slithered up Teason's spine, he heard Saul scoff before saying, "Well, at least it's not the men's room in a restaurant."

"Yessss," Jean-Paul snarled. "This is *so* much better."

Julian squeezed Teason's hip once before easing him behind him. "Stay with Saul," he ordered.

Teason wanted to protest. After all, they had swords, and the vampires were unarmed. Except, a second later, both vampires lifted their hands, and something grew from their fingernails—something that looked like several-inch long, lethal-looking claws.

Oh, you forgot to tell me something important.

That was the last thought to go through Teason's mind before the pair took on the trio in a clash of blades and claws . . . and Teason's brain checked out.

Chapter Nine

"Shit."

Julian heard Saul mutter the word softly, but he was too busy dodging a sword strike to glance the big human's way. Once he'd parried the vampire, he slipped close and rammed his claws deep into the man's ribcage, angling up. The vampire gasped and stumbled backward, off of his claws.

It wasn't a killing blow, but it took the vampire out of the fight for a moment. The guy clutched his side and snarled, but he didn't advance again, yet.

Turning his attention to Jean-Paul, Julian saw his coven master in battle with the other two men. He whirled, ducked, and dodged, all the while somehow managing to stay between the pair and their humans. As Julian started toward the closer of the two attacking vampires, he glanced Teason's way.

Seeing his sweet redhead being carried by Saul, Julian nearly faltered.

Except, Julian knew he could do nothing for whatever was wrong with his beloved until the attackers were dispatched.

Anger surged through Julian, and he channeled it into his moves. He lunged forward before slipping to his knees and sliding along the cobblestones. The stones were damp from a light sprinkle, allowing him to glide past the vampire's left side.

Julian raked the claws of one hand along the male's thigh, slicing through his femoral artery. When the vampire cried out and faltered, he jumped to his feet. With the upward movement, he slashed across the man's chest with his other hand, ending by embedding his claws in the man's jugular. Julian twisted his wrist and tore out the attacker's throat.

The vampire fell, the light leaving his eyes.

Out of the corner of his eye, Julian noticed two things. First, Jean-Paul had just managed to decapitate his remaining opponent, having stolen his sword. Second, Julian's original attacker was attempting to sneak up on the vampire master.

Sprinting past Jean-Paul, Julian engaged the already healing vampire. He dodged the vampire's clumsy strikes, getting inside his guard. Grabbing his wrists, Julian used his larger weight plus his momentum to drive him deeper into the shadows and slam him against a brick wall.

Julian leaned back when the vampire snapped his head forward, attempting to sink his fangs into his throat. With a hard press to a pressure point on the other man's wrist, he forced the vampire to drop his sword. Using the hold he still had on the attacker's wrist, Julian yanked and twisted his arm. He forced the vampire to face the wall, slamming his head into the stone.

Lifting his clawed hand to the vampire's throat, Julian wrapped them around his neck, preparing to end him.

"Wait."

Jean-Paul's voice stayed Julian's hand, but he didn't release the male. He turned his attention to his coven master. The vampire approached, using a handkerchief to clean the blood from his claws.

Behind Jean-Paul, Saul glanced around and kept close, still holding an unconscious Teason.

"What happened to Teason?" Julian demanded on a growl. It took all his discipline to continue holding their attacker when every instinct in his body urged him to go to his beloved. "Where's he injured? How bad?"

"Not injured. Just fainted," Saul told him. Flicking his attention to Julian's claws before meeting his gaze, he smirked and arched a brow. "Didn't show him your claws before?"

"Damn." Julian winced. "Forgot to explain that."

Saul shrugged his massive shoulders, not seeming to be having any trouble carrying the smaller human. "He'll probably wake up embarrassed, but that'll be all."

After a nod of acknowledgment, Julian turned his attention back to the struggling vampire. "Can I kill him now, Master?"

The vampire turned his head just enough to snarl at him, but he couldn't get free of Julian's hold.

"Not quite yet," Jean-Paul stated, tucking his handkerchief into a pocket on the inside of his suit jacket. He pinned the vampire with a cold-eyed gaze. "I want to know why you attacked us." Using a hand to indicate the two men lying dead in the alley with them, he added, "And in the middle of Paris. You run the risk of exposing us all with your foolishness. Why did you do it?" Lifting his chin, Jean-Paul gave him a haughty stare. "Don't you know who I am?"

"Course I know who you are," the vampire responded with a sneer. He managed to glance at their beloveds before curling his lip at Jean-Paul. "You're a disgrace. Bonding with a *human*. You don't deserve to lead."

"You're not part of my coven." Jean-Paul's tone turned musing. "How'd you know not only that I'd bonded with a human but where I'd be?"

The vampire spat at him, but the glob missed.

Julian used his hold on the vampire's throat to pull him back before slamming his head into the stone. "Answer the question," he ordered, then slammed his head again.

With a cackle, the vampire bargained, "Let me go, and I'll tell you all about how you're about to lose your coven." His voice lowered to a snarl. "Because you're weak."

Julian exchanged a glance with Jean-Paul.

Jean-Paul arched a brow as he returned his focus back to their attacker. "I don't think so." As he spoke, the irises of his eyes turned from their normal dark brown to a deep blood red. Quick as a flash, Jean-Paul was at their side, and he placed his palm on the vampire's head, forcing him to hold his gaze. "You will tell me *everything*."

The vampire's eyes widened, and he tried to turn his head away, but Jean-Paul and Julian held him fast. Their attacker's eyes grew wider. His jaw sagged open, and a look of horror crossed his lean features.

A second later, the vampire's eyes rolled to the back of his head, and his body went limp.

Jean-Paul released him and stepped back, saying, "Now, you may kill him."

Julian did just that, having no qualms about tearing out the unconscious vampire's throat. After dropping the male to the cobblestone ground, he tore the shirt from the vampire's back and began using it to clean his hands while focusing on Jean-Paul. "How big a problem do we have?" Julian knew that his coven master would have torn through the vampire's mind, extracting any and all useful information.

"Enforcer Antoine is attempting a coup," Master Jean-Paul stated bluntly, his attention straying to the three downed vampires strewn about the alley. "He sent these idiots to try to kill me or Saul."

"Our second enforcer?" Jean-Paul snarled, shaking his head as he stalked toward his beloved. "Damn him."

"Indeed." Jean-Paul's tone sounded mild, but Julian could hear the underlying anger in it. "Enforcers Clementine and Lourde are in on it, too, as well as several trackers." Focusing on Julian with narrowed eyes, Jean-Paul gave him a feral smile. "We'll have to clean house when we return."

"Three of our five enforcers and several trackers," Julian grumbled, feeling a twist in his gut that so many of their own would turn against them. "Whyever would they do this?"

As Julian took Teason from Saul's arms, he muttered a

thank you.

"Yeah, man." Saul patted Julian on the shoulder before slipping an arm around Jean-Paul's waist. "So, what's the play?"

Jean-Paul returned Saul's one-armed embrace. "It seems they are under the impression that humans should be treated as cattle, nothing more than blood bags," he stated, answering Julian's question first. He waved a hand negligently at the dead vampires. "These are rogues he promised a place in the coven to if they helped. They were also tasked with kidnapping several tourists so they could start their human herd."

Julian growled softly, clutching his still-unconscious beloved closer. "They want to return us to the Dark Ages," he grumbled. "What idiots."

"Yes." Jean-Paul's voice turned dry. "Idiots." With a scoff, he added, "Especially if Antione thought these morons could take us down." Heaving a sigh, Jean-Paul pulled out his phone. "Keep watch and turn away any who approach. I'll call for a clean-up crew."

Nodding, Julian moved toward the entrance of the alley. They were fortunate that the misty drizzle from earlier had driven most tourists indoors. There were few around to have noticed the attack or carnage left behind.

Julian listened to Jean-Paul speak into his phone, requesting aid from a local paranormal crew. While there wasn't a coven actually in the area, most large cities did have a group or two who would hide an altercation such as this. With the growing population of humans coupled with the increase of technology, these groups were essential in keeping the paranormal community's anonymity.

Feeling Teason stir in his arms, Julian peered down at his beloved. Adjusting his stance, he made certain his back was to the mess behind him. *Teason doesn't need to see that.* Julian watched him blink his eyes a few times before they actually focused. His brows were furrowed as he glanced around. Then he finally looked up at him.

Smiling a little, Julian murmured, "Hey, *ma adorée*. You feeling okay now?"

"Yeah, I'm okay," Teason mumbled, looking a little confused. "What happened?" Just as Julian was about to explain, Teason's eyes opened wide, and he stiffened in his arms. "Holy shit. Those men attacked us with swords, and you grew claws." Teason focused on Julian's hands where they cradled his body for a few seconds before lifting his chin to meet his gaze. "Didn't you?"

Disliking the uncertainty in Teason's tone, Julian quickly nodded. "Yes, vampires can grow claws," he told him. "I apologize that I forgot to mention it." Offering a half-shrug, Julian could only state in his defense, "There's just so much to share when it comes to the paranormal world."

Scoffing, Teason mumbled, "You got that right." Then he winced as he peered at Julian from beneath his lashes. "I fainted, didn't I?"

"So Saul told me." Julian offered his beloved a small smile. "He caught you, so at least you didn't hit your head again." Seeing the flush creeping up Teason's neck and smelling the rising scent of his embarrassment, Julian hurried to say, "I'm so sorry you ended up in a situation that caused you such stress."

Teason sighed. "I feel sorta like you should take away my man card," he grumbled. Then, waving at the ground, he muttered, "Can you put me down, please?"

"I can, but I'd rather you not look in the alley, if it's all the same to you." As Julian spoke, he maneuvered Teason to his feet. Fighting his own flush, he admitted, "I'd rather you didn't see the carnage we caused."

"You didn't cause it, I'm sure," Teason declared, but he did turn his back to the scene behind Julian. "They attacked you.

You were just defending yourself and taking care of business."

Julian really liked how Teason tucked himself up against him. Wrapping his arms around his lover, he nuzzled his face into his human's hair, inhaling deeply. Tension he hadn't realized he still carried drained from his body now that he had his beloved safe, awake, and standing in his arms.

"Thank you for your faith in me, *ma adorée*," Julian crooned before pressing a light kiss to the warm skin behind his beloved's ear.

"You'll always keep me safe," Teason whispered, glancing over his shoulder at him.

The expression of trust on Teason's features damn near caused Julian's heart to skip a beat.

"So those were vampires who attacked us, right?" Teason cuddled into Julian's embrace. "Why?"

Always wanting to be honest, Julian explained what they'd learned. Thinking of Antoine, Clementine, and Lourde's betrayal caused the food in Julian's gut to curdle. While Antoine had occasionally acted like an entitled jerk, he'd always followed orders faithfully. For him to not only speak out against the coven master, but to also convince others to join his cause, Julian couldn't wait to hand him his head.

"Guess the paranormal have their bad apples, too," Teason mused softly.

"Yes, unfortunately we do."

Before more could be said, a number of figures slipped from the shadows of the alley across the street. They carried bags and scented as a mixture of vampires and shifters.

Julian realized the cleaners had arrived.

"Time to get on with our date," Julian murmured into Teason's ear.

I hope we can still make it to the Eiffel Tower in time.

Chapter Ten

Teason had loved his time in Paris. Never in his wildest imagination would he have believed that he would actually get to go there. After three days enjoying the sights, however, they needed to head back to the coven.

From Julian, Teason had learned that Master Jean-Paul had passed on the information he'd gleaned from the rogue vampire's mind to Second Blaise. The vampire had been pissed, which sounded about right. After a long phone call together—Saul and Teason had played cards—Julian, Jean-Paul, and Blaise had set a plan in motion. Blaise had started making discreet inquiries and creating a network of people they could trust within the coven.

Teason figured that had to suck. They had to vet their own people all over again. These were people they lived with, worked with, and spent recreational time with. Teason didn't know them, but he knew the betrayal had to cut deep.

While Julian tried to hide it, Teason occasionally noticed his preoccupation. When they were in the Louvre, he'd caught his vampire staring blankly at a painting or sculpture, and he knew the man wasn't seeing it. On top of that, Julian always remained hyper-aware as they walked the streets, taking in the sights.

"Do you have everything?" Julian asked, leaning against the doorframe. His smile was filled with amusement as he watched Teason trying to zipper his suitcase. "Do you need help with that?"

Scoffing, Teason took a step back and waved at the bag.

"You're the one that insisted on buying me a million clothes while here."

Along with sightseeing, the vampires had insisted on clothes shopping for both Teason and Saul. Teason understood the need, considering he'd essentially been kidnapped from his baggage job at the airport. Saul, on the other hand, hadn't been a fan of clothes shopping. Evidently, he bought most of his stuff online and had it shipped to him. That way, he could avoid stores. Jean-Paul had to do some quick talking—or maybe it was the blowjob Teason had overheard the vampire master giving his new friend.

With a chuckle, Julian crossed to the bed. He placed one hand on the lid, making it look easy to keep it closed. Then he zipped it up.

"Freaking vampire strength," Teason grumbled good-naturedly, laughing when Julian preened. "Yeah, yeah."

"Happy to help." Julian grabbed Teason around the waist and reeled him in for a kiss.

Teason was only too happy to go, plastering himself against Julian's big body. He opened eagerly to his lover, enjoying the taste of coffee mixed with his amazing vampire. When Julian's hand landed on his ass, Teason moaned and lifted a leg, wrapping it around his body.

It still amazed him how hot Julian could make him in barely an instant.

"Not now, gentlemen." Jean-Paul's amused voice came from the doorway. "It's time to go."

Julian ended the kiss on a groan. He rested his forehead against Teason's, panting softly, sharing breaths. "Damn. What you do to me, *ma adorée*," he muttered gruffly, a smile playing around the corners of his full lips.

"Back atcha," Teason replied, barely recognizing his husky voice.

Gripping Teason's hand, Julian threaded their fingers together. "We'd best not keep the master waiting." He grabbed Teason's suitcase with his free hand. As Julian led the way out of the bedroom, he told him, "Regardless of the damn unrest at our coven, I'm still eager to show it to you." His expression turned earnest. "It's truly a beautiful place."

"I can't wait."

Teason figured the vampire could scent the truth in his words, for he grinned widely, showing off his fangs. Just seeing those pointy teeth caused a warmth to unfurl in his belly . . . again. Never in a million years would Teason have imagined him with a biting fetish, but for his vampire, he did.

Julian groaned, giving his hand a squeeze. "Later, Teason," he muttered. "On the plane."

Anticipation thrummed through Teason.

"Oh, god, Julian," Teason moaned, arching into each of his vampire's hard thrusts. "Yesssss."

Julian growled. "Love the fucking sounds you make," he declared, driving into Teason's body over and over.

Teason groaned again, sparks lighting up his nerve endings. The prick of Julian's fingernails digging into the flesh of his hips set off a fresh wave of tingles over his skin. His groin felt hot, and his cock throbbed with the beat of his heart.

Every thrust of Julian's thick erection sinking into Teason's body felt better than the last. His vampire skillfully pegged his gland with every punching rut. The way Julian's heavy balls slapped against his own sent scintillating zings through them.

"C-Close," Teason warned. He dug his fingers into the back of the chair his stomach was draped over. "Oh, gods, so close."

"Yessss, do it, *ma adorée,*" Julian demanded, bending over him and pressing his strong chest against Teason's sweat-dampened backside. "Come for your vampire."

Then Julian wrapped his right arm around Teason's torso and, with unerring precision, gripped his nipple and gave it a pinch.

That last flash of sensation pushed Teason barreling over the edge. He screamed his pleasure as his balls unloaded. His semen burst from him in ecstasy-inducing jolts, painting the cushion of the chair he was kneeling on.

"Fuck!" Julian roared, slamming into Teason one last time. His arms came around him, clutching him close as his body shuddered behind him.

Teason felt Julian's prick swell just a smidge within him, the feeling indescribable. The hot jets of cum Julian pulsed into him heated him from the inside out. His body shaking with the intensity of his release, Teason still managed to tilt his head in invitation.

With a groan, Julian gave Teason what he wanted, what they both needed. He sank his fangs into Teason's flesh and drank. The sensation of Julian sucking on his neck transferred straight to his cock, yanking him over the edge once more.

Crying Julian's name, Teason fought against the spots threatening at the edges of his vision. He panted hard as the bliss went on and on. Teason floated with pleasure, barely registering when Julian eased his teeth from his neck.

Feeling his vampire lap at his flesh, Teason smiled. He turned his head as far as he could, and Julian granted him a deep, languorous kiss. Teason tasted his blood on Julian's tongue, and a deep well of satisfaction filled him that he was the one to take care of his vampire's needs.

"*Ma adorée,*" Julian crooned, nuzzling his lips against Teason's temple. "I am so very grateful I stumbled upon you with your baggage cart."

Teason chuckled softly. "Me, too."

Julian slowly eased his softening prick from his chute, and

Teason sighed deeply. While he knew it was necessary, there was always a part of him that wished his vampire could stay right there, seated within him, all the time. Considering that wasn't practical, Teason never said anything.

"Stay still, beloved," Julian encouraged, rubbing over his back. "I'll get something to clean us up."

Still kneeling on the soft cushioned chair, Teason did as his vampire bid. He rested his weight on his forearms and sighed as he watched the big sexy male stride down the plane's narrow aisle. The flex and relax of Julian's hard ass cheeks called to him, and Teason wanted to squeeze them in the worst way.

Julian stopped at the small kitchenette area and wet a cloth, his medium-bronze skin rippling over his firm muscles.

Teason truly believed his vampire was a damn Adonis, and he wondered how he'd ended up so lucky.

When Julian turned, Teason got a real good view of his thick, half-hard prick, still damp from the slick they'd used. His ass clenched, and his mouth watered. He knew from experience in the hotel room that if he were to play with that beautiful piece of meat, he could get Julian hard again, starting another round.

Groaning, Julian shook his head as he returned to his side. "Not this time, *ma adorée,*" he stated regretfully. "I hear Jean-Paul and Saul finishing up in the bedroom." Julian bent and dropped a kiss to Teason's shoulder as he began using the damp cloth to clean him up. "We need to dress."

Jean-Paul and Saul had commandeered the bedroom for their short flight from Paris to Montpellier. The master had wanted to fuck his beloved in a bed at thirty-thousand feet. That hadn't stopped Julian and Teason from doing the same, just as his vampire had promised him. They'd just commandeered a very comfortable chair.

Once Julian had cleaned them both up, Teason grabbed his clothes and pulled them on. He noticed Julian using another cloth to wipe down the seat cushions. Teason couldn't quite fight the bit of heat that began rising up his neck.

Damn fair skin and freckles.

Once all visual evidence of their tryst had been erased, Julian settled in a seat beside Teason on a small loveseat. He wrapped his arm around his shoulders and pulled him close, nuzzling Teason's neck. Teason listened as Julian told him a bit more about the coven as they waited for their companions to exit the bedroom.

It wasn't until the pilot alerted them to their impending descent that Jean-Paul opened the door and led a clearly sated Saul out of the room. When the big human took a seat, he shifted a little, obviously searching for a comfortable position. Jean-Paul wore a smugly satisfied look.

In short order, the plane landed safely, and they disembarked. A man and a woman stood off to the side next to a limousine. Another man wielded a baggage cart, and he began helping the pilot with the luggage.

With a hand on his back, Julian guided Teason toward the couple near the vehicle. Before they'd even reached it, the pair were smiling, welcoming Jean-Paul and Julian home.

"Thank you, Camille, Marcel," Jean-Paul replied with a smile. "It is very good to be home." His expression hardened. "Even with what we're walking into."

"Yes, Master Jean-Paul," Camille responded, her full lips curving down with displeasure. Julian had told Teason that she was one of their coven's enforcers—one that they still trusted. "I hear the rat is making his move upon our return."

"Good," Jean-Paul replied in a hard tone. "Best to get it over with."

"Your beloveds will be kept safe, sirs," Marcel commented softly before moving his gaze over Jean-Paul's shoulder. The tall, lean vampire was considered a coven guard and was one of Jean-Paul's regular drivers. "I'll load the luggage if you want to get comfortable."

"Thank you." Jean-Paul turned toward the rear door that Camille had opened. "And thank you, Camille."

"It's my honor, sir," she replied, panning her gaze over the hanger in a way that was eerily similar to how Julian always did it.

Huh. Maybe he trained her.

Once settled in the limo's seat beside Julian and the door was closed, Saul asked what Teason had been wondering. "So, what did Enforcer Camille mean when she said the rat is making his move?" The big blond rested his hand on Jean-Paul's thigh, a look of concern marring his usually relaxed features. "What are we walking into?"

Jean-Paul scoffed softly even as he threaded his fingers through his lover's blond hair. "Two options. Antoine will challenge me the second I walk in the door, or he'll try to attack us unawares."

"You really think he'll go the honorable approach?" Julian asked dryly. He tightened his arm around Teason's shoulders, tucking him close to his side.

Teason was more than happy to stay snuggled against him.

Staring at his head enforcer, Jean-Paul gave him a droll look. "The vampire's an idiot, remember?" His smile appeared feral. "After all, I'm weak for bonding with a human. He just might think he can beat me."

"In that case, this'll be easy," Julian declared with a scoff.

Teason wondered if it could really be that easy.

Chapter Eleven

Just as Julian had feared, it wasn't that easy.

When they walked into the coven, Julian could feel the slight tremors working down Teason's body through the palm he had on his beloved's back. He rubbed up and down his spine, doing his best to soothe him. Julian knew that if he could smell the nerves his sweet human was feeling, then every vampire in the place could, too.

Fortunately, upon hearing the welcoming calls from every person they passed, Julian felt Teason begin to relax.

Good.

"Welcome home, Jean-Paul." Second Blaise's voice boomed through the hallway as he strode toward them. "It's a pleasure to have you back."

Out of the corner of his eye, Julian spotted Teason's lips part, and his nerves turned to shock. He barely refrained from allowing his lips to twitch in a smirk. Julian figured he really should have warned his beloved.

Blaise was a big black vampire, standing six-foot-seven. He was the hammer to Julian's surgical blade. Master Jean-Paul knew how to utilize both of their talents with precision.

Which was exactly why Antoine wouldn't see them coming because Blaise would normally go at something full steam ahead. Instead, Julian had spent hours on the phone with the big man walking him through his own subtle, behind-the-scenes approach. That way, Antoine would never expect they were onto him, even though his half-ass assassins never checked in.

"And welcome back to you, too, Julian." Blaise shook both their hands. "You've been missed."

Master Jean-Paul dipped his chin in a small nod, a smile curving his lips. "Thank you, Blaise." After shaking his second's hand, he wrapped his arm back around Saul. "I'd like you to meet my beloved, Saul Mandisa." Smiling wryly, Jean-Paul claimed, "I had the great fortune to meet him my first evening in Vegas."

"Congratulations to you both." Blaise smiled broadly, showing off even white teeth in his black face. He didn't offer his hand to Saul as he told him, "Welcome to the coven. Whatever we can do to make you more comfortable, let us know."

"Thank you, uh, Blaise." Saul nodded a bit as he added, "Good to be here."

"And I hear you met your beloved on your last day there." Blaise chuckled as he took in Teason. "Lucky you."

Julian tightened his arm just a little with a scoff. "Yes, my most fortunate day there." He pecked a kiss to Teason's temple before returning his attention to the vampire he'd considered his friend for over one hundred years. "This is Teason Lofgren."

"Welcome to you, too, Teason." After Teason murmured his thanks, Blaise refocused on their master. "I noticed Camille and Marcel are taking your luggage to your rooms. When do you want to debrief?" Blaise hesitated a couple of heartbeats before saying, "We received a message from the Vampire Council this morning that I'd like to go over with you."

"Really?" Jean-Paul hummed. "Interesting." He glanced around, and Julian knew that his master was noticing the same thing he did . . . there were plenty of vampires loitering. "Why don't you meet me in my study in an hour and a half. That'll give us time to shower off the stink of travel."

Blaise chuckled low in his throat as he leaned forward and

sniffed at them both—none-too-discreetly. "And maybe wash off something else, too."

"Shut up," Jean-Paul snarled, but there was no heat in the sound.

With a snort, Blaise took a step back and turned. "See you in a bit." As he began walking away, a grin still on his face, he called over his shoulder, "It really is good to have you back. Maybe I should go to Vegas soon."

"Come on," Jean-Paul urged, moving forward. "That means you only have an hour and a half, too."

"Figured as much." Julian moved his hand to grip Teason's, threading their fingers together and giving them a squeeze. "Let me show you our suite here."

To Julian's relief, Teason smiled and nodded. He was also pleased that his beloved had relaxed.

"This place can be a little bit of a maze," Jean-Paul was telling Saul as he led the way past the central stairs to an elevator in the hall to the right. "This is the most central elevator," he explained, hitting the button for the fourth floor, which was the top level. "If you're not sure where it is, ask any vampire here, and they'll direct you."

Saul arched a brow. While he didn't look like he believed the master—not that Julian blamed him, all things considered—the big human still nodded.

After riding the elevator to their floor, Jean-Paul led the way to the left. "The top floor contains three suites. Mine"—he pointed to the left—"Julian's"—he pointed to the right—"and Blaise's at the back of the house." On the last name, Jean-Paul pointed behind them. "Opposite Blaise's is our private offices, a library, and a conference room."

Both Saul and Teason nodded.

"Can we explore?" Saul asked, glancing around curiously. "Wander room from room to figure out where everything is?"

"As long as the door isn't locked," Jean-Paul told his beloved with a smile. "If it is"—he punched in a number on the keypad next to his door, unlocking it—"it means it's someone's private residence."

"Got it." Saul followed Jean-Paul into their suite, grabbing one of the suitcases that someone had left at their door. After all, Camille and Marcel wouldn't enter without permission. "No intruding on private space. Cool."

"You won't need to worry about that, *human*," a deep-voiced male snarled from within the room they were entering. *Antoine*. "Because you'll only be let into a room if you're needed. Otherwise, *human*, you'll be locked in your stall, where you belong."

Julian couldn't help but notice that Antoine made the word human sound like a curse.

Idiotic, since he needs them to survive.

Several more vampires appeared—two from the service elevator, one from Julian's own room, and another pair from the elevator they'd just vacated. They all held guns in their hands as they clustered around them. After glancing at them, Jean-Paul moved into his room, drawing Saul in behind him. Julian quickly followed, keeping Teason as close to his back as possible.

"Ah, Antoine. The rule does apply to you, too." Jean-Paul didn't sound in the least bit surprised. "You really shouldn't be snooping around my quarters."

"Not snooping. Just deciding how to remodel," Antoine countered with a curl of his lips. "These rooms'll be mine very soon."

Jean-Paul arched one brow imperiously, not looking the least bit impressed. "Are you issuing a formal challenge, Antoine?"

"Don't have to," Antoine claimed, glancing at the vampires who filed in behind them. "'Cause I got their support." With a cold chuckle, he crossed his arms over his chest. "They can't wait for when they can take their rightful place at the top of the food chain and put humans in theirs."

"Blah, blah, blah," Jean-Paul toned, obviously shocking Antoine. The other vampire gaped as the vampire master actually rolled his eyes, looking completely unimpressed. "Just shut up, Antione. I don't need to know your evil plan."

"How dare you speak to me that—" Antoine began to roar, stalking close and pointing a finger in the master's face.

Jean-Paul continued in a moderate, dry tone. "Because I already know it."

Quick as a striking rattlesnake, Jean-Paul snapped his hand out. His claws extended in that instant, and he sank them into Antoine's neck. Curling them and tugging, Jean-Paul used the hold to not only tear out Antoine's throat, but yank the dying vampire close, using him as a shield for himself and Saul . . . just in case.

Saul must have missed the memo, for as soon as he saw Jean-Paul move, he lunged at the vampire to Antoine's left—Tracker Lorie. With a move that looked way too smooth and practiced, he relieved the vampire of her weapon. In the next instant, Saul stood at Jean-Paul's back, pointing the gun at Lorie.

Julian saw it all even as he pushed Teason to the floor with the hold on his neck. Jumping forward, he grabbed Clementine by the throat, lifted her from the ground, and swung her like a bat. Julian pivoted, slamming her feet into two of the other vampires in the room and knocking them to the floor.

Removing the gun from Clementine, Julian dropped her before shooting her in the head. He lifted the weapon and pointed it at the only other standing male—ex-enforcer Lourde. To the man's credit, he dropped his weapon and lifted his arms.

A second later, the tell-tale beep of buttons being pushed on the keypad outside reached Julian's ears.

Blaise rushed into the room followed by several guards and trackers, only to pull up short when both Julian and Saul pointed their guns at them. The second swept his gaze over the room, amazement filling his dark expression. Julian lowered his gun, Saul following suit, so Blaise pointed at the vampires who were still living.

"Take them into custody," Blaise ordered. As those behind him moved, he shook his head as he surveyed the room again. "Damn. I was really hoping to help kick ass." His brows shot up as he spotted Saul with the gun and Lorie on the floor, massaging fingers that looked like they might be broken. "Damn. How'd you manage that?"

Saul scoffed. "Used to work for some illegal assholes a few years ago. Self-defense was a necessity in order to stay safe and get out."

Blaise jerked a nod. "Nice. We'll start you in training so you know more about fighting vampires."

Grinning, Saul rumbled, "Thanks, man."

Jean-Paul growled softly, glancing between them. "I don't want my beloved in danger or hurt."

Unrepentant, Blaise shrugged. "Then he needs to know how to defend himself even better than he can now." The huge vampire second shook his head. "It's a dangerous world, Master."

"Can I learn, too?"

Hearing his beloved's voice, Julian pivoted, shoving the gun into a pocket. He quickly helped Teason to his feet. "I'm so sorry, *ma adorée,*" he murmured, running his hands over his sexy human's body. "I didn't hurt you when I pushed you, did I?" Julian never wanted to hurt the other half of his soul. "I just needed you safe."

Relatively.

To Julian's relief, Teason smiled broadly as he stared up at him. "I understand, and I'm not hurt." He stood on his toes and pecked a kiss to Julian's lips. Then he focused on Blaise again. "And I'm serious. I want to learn, too."

"That would be wise," Blaise told him, ignoring Julian when he growled at the second. Instead, he glanced around the room. "We'll have this cleaned up in ten if you want to head to the bathroom, Master Jean-Paul."

"Thank you, Blaise." Jean-Paul glanced around his front sitting room. "Think this was all of them?"

"We'll continue to research everyone," Julian assured, tucking Teason against his chest. "In the meantime." He sighed. "I may not like it, but yes, training our beloveds would be best."

Jean-Paul growled, but he nodded. "I understand." Gripping Saul's free hand, he muttered, "After all, I heard from my friends that some shifters arm their human mates with tranquilizer guns." Then Jean-Paul stalked deeper into his home, disappearing from sight.

Huh. Now there's an idea.

Still, Teason will need to know how to buy himself enough time to be able to use the weapon.

"Come on, *ma adorée*," Julian encouraged, moving past the vampires securing those involved in the attempted coup. "Time for that shower." He couldn't help the low growl as he added, "And I may need to inspect every inch of your body for injury."

To Julian's amusement—and pleasure—Teason pinned him with a narrow, hungry look and purred, "Oh, I'm counting on it."

Julian growled as he picked Teason up and tossed him over his shoulder. He heard his beloved laugh and smacked a hand over his ass to hold him in place. Sprinting from the room, Julian ignored the chuckles from his fellow vampires in favor of getting to his own suite . . . then the bathroom.

As Julian stripped Teason's clothes from him, he loved the way his human didn't resist. He knew his beloved understood. And while Julian never wanted to see his human in danger again, he understood that life happened, so there was always that possibility.

Together we'll face it, and we'll be stronger for it.

Those were the ties that bonding with his fated one promised him . . . and Julian looked forward to every blessed second of it.

About the Author

Charlie started writing fantasy when she was eight, and after stumbling onto her first erotic romance at age nineteen, she realized her true calling. She now focuses on writing gay erotic romance, normally of the paranormal variety, with heroes of all kinds. With the help and support of her husband, Charlie finally fulfilled one of her life-long goals . . . move to acreage with her horses. You can often find her curled up with her laptop and a cup of tea or glass of wine, creating her next adventure. Charlie enjoys exploring the mountains of her new Oregon home on horseback, 4-wheeler, or motorcycle.

She can be reached at ch.richards2010@yahoo.com

Or visit her at www.charlie-richards.com.

www.ingramcontent.com/pod-product-compliance
Lightning Source LLC
LaVergne TN
LVHW020654100826
845148LV00012B/2495
* 9 7 8 1 4 8 7 4 3 9 4 1 5 *